Cover: Dynasty Cover Me
Editor: LDS Literary Services
Proofreader: Brandi Jordan

BLACKINK
PUBLICATIONS

D0684357

Dedication

All praise is for Allah, alone. Dedicated to the love of my life and best friend, she knows who she is, to my mother Deidra, my grandmother Rainey, and my children, Jessica, Ervin and Ramel.

The Dark Prince:
Prince of Darkness
A Novel By
Sa'id Salaam

PROLOGUE

"Show time, shawty!" Meechie called and knocked on the dressing room door. His newest client was his ticket to the big leagues, but he was starting to be a lot of work. Like most entertainers, he had a thing for the ladies. To be fair, the ladies loved him back.

Prince stood a muscular, dark chocolate 6' 1" with even darker eyes. He had a hypnotic effect that seemed to affect both men and women alike. He was a natural born leader who people loved to be near. Yes, he was destined to be a star if his manager, Meechie, could get him out of the dressing room.

"Come on, Prince! Let's do this shit!" the man pleaded. He was Prince's opposite, standing a squat 5'6" and tipping the scales at 225. The ladies didn't dig him like they did his client.

That's why he was grateful to have Angela in his life. She and their baby girl was his universe. That's why he went so hard to be successful. He knew his woman was running out of patience with his musical equivalent of hoop dreams. She understood the riches at stake but wouldn't mind eating a steak as it was taking so long.

In the meanwhile, it was her putting chicken on the table. Literally, since she slung hot chicken and biscuits in a fast food joint. It paid the bills and allowed her to bring plenty home, but it would be nice if he did the same.

Her strong work ethic gave her leverage to ask her boss to give him a job. He initially refused since he wanted to fuck her, but her persistence wore him down. Now he might get a favor in return and get to fuck her, as long as he fucked her.

"Come on, bruh," he shouted and pounded on the door. He tried the knob again, but it was as locked as it was two minutes ago.

"Shit!" Prince fussed, as well. He had cause to complain since he was almost inside the young woman's mouth. They were making out hot and heavy and he unzipped his zipper to introduce her to his dick. It was just as dark and handsome as he was.

"Too bad you gotta go," she teased, running her tongue around his swollen dick head. She squeezed the thick shaft and gave it a few strokes. Meanwhile, he ran his tongue up her thick jugular veins. He could feel, smell, and taste the blood coursing through her. That's why he selected her from the group of the girls she came with. They were all cute and barely dressed, but it was she he could smell. A dense, coppery smell he could taste in the air like a snake.

"I guess," Prince conceded as Meechie moaned and knocked on the door. He tucked his dick away while she put her firm breast back in her bra.

"I'm on my period anyway, but I'll give you some head after the show. Okay?" she asked needlessly. In her nineteen years, no one has said no to head yet. He would not be the first.

"You suck me and I'll suck you," he offered and stood. It didn't make sense since she just told him she was bleeding, but she wouldn't stop him if that's what he liked. She did just smoke his weed, so it was whatever.

"That's what up, shawty. Say my name when you on stage so I can stunt on my friends. Them hoes gone be tight!"

"That's what's up," he agreed. Luckily, it was tatted on her neck because he didn't ask and she didn't offer. In these days, it's easier to get some ass than a name. "Shay-Shay, right?"

"Un huh!" she eagerly agreed, nodding her heavily weaved head up and down. She popped up and posed for a quick selfie. Now when he blew up, she could brag that she sucked his dick. Crude as it may be, it was a badge of honor for a groupie. If not for her cycle, she would let him fuck without protection in hopes of getting knocked up. The best she could hope for was to swallow and hope for a miracle.

"The fuck!" Meechie griped when the door finally opened. He immediately changed his tone and cowered under his larger than life presence. "I mean, they are waiting on you shawty! We finna turn this shit out!"

That's what's up," Prince agreed.

It was the round man's enthusiasm that made him deal with him in the first place. Meechie had a cousin who made it out of their

6

southwest Atlanta hood by slinging mediocre lyrics. Prince was the real deal, though. Not only could he rap like Bun B and Andre 3000 in one, but the boy could sing. Not back up, off key type singing like most rappers. Dude had range like the late great Prince. That's how he came to be called Prince but not why. He went by The Dark Prince as homage to his real hero, mentor, and idol.

Meechie handed him a cordless mic and led the way to the stage. Prince immediately began crooning acapella, showing off his range. The girl was directed back to the club and joined her friends. The singing without seeing made for a dramatic entrance. The beautiful man didn't disappoint when he came into view.

The light reflected brilliantly off his diamond and platinum jewelry as well as the rings of waves on his head. A menacing scowl showed off a set of platinum fangs that glinted dangerously.

He had the look, could sing but when he launched into his bars it was clear he was the real deal. Meechie looked up at the VIP section and saw the look on his cousin's face. He wanted to rush onstage, grab the mic and scream 'told you so!' He settled for him nodding with his bottom lip poked out. He was willing to bet they would let him in the VIP now.

"This next one is for my girl, Shay-Shay," Prince announced and went into a song that put one in the mind of L.L cool J's vintage, "I Need Love."

"Told y'all! I told y'all bitches!" she gloated.

She broke into an end zone dance like she just scored a touchdown. Later she would blow her breath in their faces to smell semen just like youngsters do, letting friends smell their finger when they played in some pussy.

Meechie had everything riding on tonight. There would be no tomorrow if his client didn't kill it tonight. He begged his cousin, Dirt, and a few label types to come see his latest project.

They'd been down this road before and let him know this would be the last trip. If this one flopped like the others flopped, he would be dead. Not to mention he promised his woman he would get a job if this one didn't work out. He would go back to managing Micky D's instead of artists. Two minutes into the show, it was clear. The entire club, patrons, bartenders, and bouncers all froze and stared at the man on stage.

"Thank you!" Prince said and took a bow when he concluded his brief set. There was an awkward silence while everyone tried to process what they'd just witnessed. Had crickets been present, they would clearly be heard over the deafening silence. It was a brief uncomfortable moment for both, man and manager.

"That's what the fuck I'm talking 'bout!" Dirt screamed, causing the club to erupt.

It literally exploded in applause and claps. Even Shay-Shay felt like a star since she had a date with his dick. Her friends would have killed her on the spot to take her place. Ironic really, considering who he was.

"You kilt that shit, shawty!" Meechie cheered as Prince exited stage left. He wrapped him in a hug so tight, even he knew was too much. "My bad."

"You cool. What yo' people say?" Prince asked. He initially resisted the man's claims of making him rich and famous.

Meechie had heard Prince crooning on the train one night and moved on him. Prince had a couple of cars but often rode MARTA to hunt for the young girls he liked to feed on. The truants who liked to skip school, smoke weed and fuck.

The dumb girls who were smart enough to know they didn't need an education for their future careers as baby mamas and welfare recipients.

Meechie convinced him that with his contacts, he could make him a super star. He even called his cousin Dirt on the spot to prove he knew the man. He put the brief, curt call on speaker as proof. Dirt said "yeah, yeah bring him to the next showcase"

When he told him about how many women he would pull he reluctantly agreed. After all, that's why he was on the bus singing

9

in the first place. Young girls took notice and he took them home. He gave them weed, beer and dick in exchange for them quenching his insatiable thirst.

"We 'bout to find out!" he declared and began marching towards the VIP section.

He made this trip many times in the past but never got passed the velvet rope. The bouncer twisted his lips like "here we go again" when he saw him approaching. Dirt saw him too, but more importantly, the man he had in tow.

"Let them in, shawty!" Dirt stood and shouted from his booth full of champagne and groupies. They go together like peanut butter and jelly.

"But you said..." the confused man replied. Dirt had told him on several occasions not to let him in no matter how much he whined. Sure, he would tell their grandmother but he still wasn't getting in.

Dirt saw the potential in the man and wanted in. Every artist wants a label, so they could eat off an artist like their label ate off them. He would definitely sign this dude and kick his cousin to the curb. Fuck him and grandma. This dude is a gold mine.

"He with me," Meechie said of Prince coming up behind him. He couldn't wait to say those important words important people got to say. The man opened his mouth to say something but something in Prince's eyes to shut him up.

"Come on in," the bouncer said to Prince sensing he was the very important person and Meechie was with him. Even at six feet six inches, the bouncer looked up to him.

"Shawty, Shawty!" Dirt cheered animatedly. His theatrics and clowning is what got him noticed, but this dude was good. Real good and he knew it. "Shawty, you dope! Fuck with me and I'ma make you famous!"

"You gotta holla at me! I'm his manager!" Meechie announced proudly. Dirt frowned skeptically and turned to Prince for confirmation. Prince learned many moons ago it was sometimes better to listen instead of speaking in new situations. He nodded and shrugged, putting the spotlight back on Meechie.

"Damn, cuz. You got you something here! Fuck with me in the morning and let's get in the studio," Dirt said greedily. He would offer to put him on a song, but used one of the bangers he just performed, making it his own. "Grab a glass, Prince. Drink up!"

"'Preciate it, but I can't stay long," he replied, accepting a flute of champagne. The group of groupies batted their false eyelashes and laughed out loud, vying for his attention. Even if he hadn't just killed it on the stage, the man was drop dead gorgeous.

"Where you from, shawty?" Dirt inquired. He wanted to get to know the man who could make him millions.

"East side," Meechie answered for him. He did that for the next few minutes until prince rose to leave.

"Hit me tomorrow," he needlessly advised his manager. Meechie was definitely going to him tomorrow. He would have slept at the foot of his bed if he could.

"Hell yeah!" he shouted to prove it. The men and women at the table watched the man leave long after he was gone. It took that long for the spell to wear off. He swooped in and plucked Shay-Shay from her cackling crew and whisked her out of the club.

They got into his Lexus and pulled away, leaving Meechie without a ride. Dirt suddenly saw his worth and would gladly drop him off. That and whatever else he needed until he could separate him from his client.

"You were fiyah up there on stage!" Shay announced setting off pre-fuck conversation. She wished she could have met him two days earlier before her cycle so she could get that hunk of meat inside of her. That was okay, though, because she planned to suck it so good he would come back for more.

The conversation lasted until they pulled up to a rundown motel. He could afford more but it suite his needs. She had fucked here before and saw nothing wrong with it. A scruffy goon saw the shiny car pull in and immediately moved on it.

"Get us a room," Prince ordered, handing her a fresh hundred-dollar bill. She

12

saw the thug approaching and jumped out of the car. Either way, it was a win for her since she had money in hand. The man had a gun in his when he ran up.

"You know wha—" he began but got trapped in the quick sand of Prince's eyes. It started out as a jack move but now he forgot why he was there. "Umm?"

"You came to give me your money," Prince told him. He looked deep into his eyes and spoke directly to his soul.

"Fa sho!" he agreed and shoved his hand into his dirty jeans. He grabbed the few crumbled bills and pushed them forward. "Thank you."

"Nah, thank you, playa," Prince laughed and walked away. Shay returned with an old school room key instead of card and off they went.

"Got some more weed?" she wisely asked. The girl knew to get all she could upfront since her stock would drastically reduce once he bust a nut. Pussy is far more valuable before the deed than after.

"Un huh," he replied and pulled out another neatly rolled blunt. She took it and lit it, taking feverish pulls while he undressed. Halfway through the blunt, she halfheartedly offered him some. He took a pull and passed it back. It was just for show since weed and alcohol had absolutely no effect on him.

"I see you ready!" Shay laughed when she finished the blunt and saw Prince lying on his back completely naked. His thick dick laid between his legs like a third. She quickly came out of everything except her panties since she wore a pad. Prince inhaled deeply, savoring the smell of a woman.

She crawled on the bed headed straight between his legs. His dick throbbed to life as she drew near. He was semi erect when he entered her hot mouth.

"Lemme see," he said pushing her weave aside so he could watch. A good blowjob is equal parts sights, sound, and feel. Her slurps of the sloppy head matched up perfectly with the suction and she locked eyes.

"Mmhm," Shay-Shay agreed when she felt the familiar twitching of an impending orgasm. It granted him permission to come in her mouth. She grabbed his shaft and stroked until he erupted in her mouth.

"Drink up!" he ordered as she swallowed in loud gulps. She sucked him dry until he began to deflate in her mouth. "My turn!"

"I got my period," she reminded. "You can still fuck if you want to."

"Oh, I don't mind a little blood," he said, pulling her panties off. The girl didn't have much shame, but felt weird with a man seeing her monthly flow up close and personal.

She felt even weirder when he began kissing her inner thighs. He ran his tongue up the femoral artery, feeling the flow of blood. The slight flow from her vagina could not be ignored, so he didn't ignore it.

"You tripping, Bruh!" she protested when he licked her leaking labia. He ignored the complaints and clamped his mouth around her lips.

Prince sucked the flow like nectar of a ripe mango. Given the choice he'd take blood over nectar any day. In fact, it was his nectar, what he lived for. Shay began to moan and move as the sensation became sensational. An orgasm snuck up on her and shook her soul. It was a going away present from the generous man. With a quick move, he turned and clamp onto her thigh.

The super sharp fangs entered her flesh so smoothly, the pain took a few seconds to register.

"Mother fucker is you biting me! Ow! stop!" she pleaded in futility. At that moment, he was a wild animal at feeding time. She tried to push his head away but couldn't. He brutally shoved her legs so wide her hips came out of their sockets with a sickening crunch. Panic set in and she began punching his head with both hands. "Get off me, nigga!"

The extra moving and thrashing played right into his plans. Her increased heart rate sped blood coursing through her body that much quicker. Soon she felt light-headed from the loss of blood. He kept on sucking until she passed out. He kept right on going until she passed away.

"Delicious!" Prince told the corpse as a post mortem thanks. He stood and walked into the bathroom. After a quick shower, he dressed and stepped outside into the warm Atlanta night.

Dawn wasn't far off so it was time to get home. The dark Prince was the Prince of darkness and didn't do daytime. Then again what vampires do?

CHAPTER 1

Prince was born in the year 1946 on the west side of Atlanta, during a tumultuous time in the south. A time when a nigga was a nigger and called one right to his face like it was his name. The politically correct term was negro according to the signs directing which water fountain or bathroom he could use.

His parents named him Martin Jones and raised him in a good southern Baptist household. There was no smoking, drinking, dancing, or loud talking in the Jones home. Mother Margaret would clamp her own hand over her mouth when father Walter would lay some pipe. Missionary position of course, but he still heard them. When lovemaking gets good, it turns into some fucking whether they liked it or not.

Walter was a far cry from the glamorous men who courted the pretty Haitian girl back in Haiti or when she came to America. She sang in saloons and bars for drunken sailors at the age of fifteen. By sixteen, she was turning tricks even though she didn't know any magic. One sailor brought her to America only to discard her for another girl. That's when she met Walter. He was dark and rough but sweet and hard working. After growing up in a third world country, she eagerly accepted the security the older man offered.

He married her and put a baby in her right away. He planned to have ten children but God is the best of planners, so all they got was

Martin. He was plenty though and made his family proud. Prince excelled in school and sports and was well liked. A loving child with a good heart.

By age 13, he stood his full six foot one inches tall and a good nine inches long. He got his chocolate good looks and wavy hair from his beautiful Haitian mother. The broad shoulders and muscular frame came from his hard working daddy as well as a deep baritone voice, making him a standout in the church choir. That and his chocolate good looks and muscular frame, of course.

The church women batted eyes and openly flirted with the teen. Only when his protective mother wasn't around since she would read them the riot act in French whenever she caught them hovering around her only child. They couldn't understand the beautiful language but caught the angry tone loud and clear.

By sixteen, there was nothing she could do to keep her son out of the girls. The ladies loved him long before they loved Cool J and he loved them back. She just turned a blind eye and pretended not to notice or know.

Life was good. They lived in a nice home with a nice car and all bills were paid. Yes, life was good until it went bad.

*****

"I don't know why your daddy is so late," Margaret fussed when the clock struck six PM. The factory let out at five and the drive was

18

only twenty minutes. A half hour on a bad day, but today was the worst day. As usual, she muttered something in French like she did whenever she was upset. Her husband never learned the language of love which suite her just fine. That allowed her to sass him and make it sound sweet. Prince never took the time to learn the language either.

"Traffic," Prince tossed, out hoping she would agree and tell him to go on and start eating. The table was set, the food was cooked but nothing got eaten until the patriarch took his place at the head of the table and said his grace.

"Traffic in Atlanta is not that bad!" she shot back. Prince would remember that statement fifty years later once the city grew by hundreds of thousands of new comers and transplants. Now traffic was as bad, if not worse than New York or Los Angeles.

"Yes ma'am, I—" he began but a knock on the door interrupted him. He stood to go answer it since his mother never would. She was too prim and proper to talk to strange men on her doorstep or anywhere else for that matter.

"Jones residence?" a black police officer asked when Prince opened the door.

"Yes but my father isn't in yet," he explained. The sudden change on the man's face explained why. He removed his policeman's hat and placed it over his heart before he spoke.

"I'm sorry to inform you, but there's been an accident," he began. Margaret listened on from the corner and felt her knees buckle at the bad news. It only got worse when the policeman's mouth opened again.

"Is he okay?" Prince asked and assumed the best. His father was Superman and there wasn't any kryptonite in Atlanta, so he had to be.

"No. He passed away. I'm sorry," he said solemnly. Both were startled by a high-pitched scream that pierced their very souls. The cop had more information but it would have to wait since he went to attend to his mother.

"Mom," Prince called as his mother sank to the floor below. He tried to lift her up but she gained three hundred pounds of grief. The woman was inconsolable over the loss of her soul mate.

"Excuse me?" the policeman called as he stepped tentatively inside. He stuck his head around the corner to deliver the rest of the information since the body had to be claimed. Margaret's thick legs had spread in her grief, allowing him to look all the way up to her white, cotton bloomers.

"Yes?" Prince said and stepped in front to guard his mother's modesty and took down what needed to be done next.

The cop was gone for over an hour before hunger forced the grieving family to eat. Fried chicken is good cold or hot, so neither registered the change in temperature. The breadwinner who provided the bread and meat was no more and that weighed heavily on their minds. Now he was gone.

*****

When it first rained on the earth, it poured and it always will. Same with bad news and misfortune that comes like waves. If Walter dying in an automobile wreck wasn't bad enough, it would get worse. The insurance adjuster came to the house two days later, bearing more bad news instead of a much needed check.

"Mrs. Jones?" the man greeted and smiled as Prince let him inside. He cast a glance around much like a robber would do. They didn't have many black customers who paid their life insurance policies like Mr. Jones.

"Thanks for coming so quickly. We have to pay for his funeral today or they will turn him over to the city," Mrs. Jones sighed with relief. No one wants their loved one buried in a cardboard box in a potters field.

"Well, there is a small problem," he said and produced the police report. He slid it over the coffee to table and let her read it for herself. He had wondered if the negro woman could read while he made his way to the house. When her face twisted and contorted at the good part, he knew she read just fine.

"I don't believe this!" she insisted when she read that a known prostitute died along with her husband in the car. The impact caused her to bite the tip of his dick off and resulted in him getting a ticket for unsafe driving. Head can be just as intoxicating as liquor and distracted him enough to cross the centerline and collide with a truck.

"The driver of the other vehicle was badly injured and will have extensive medical bills as well as disability, so his insurance company will file claims against your husband's estate," he explained. He left out the part about them having the same insurance company.

"Estate? What estate? We can't even bury him without the payout!" Mrs. Jones moaned. It wasn't quite true since Mr. Jones had a few grand hidden away in the closet because he didn't trust the bank.

"Well, I'm sure something can be worked out," the adjuster said and stood.

"Thank you, sir," she said and escorted him to the door. He left with a smile but retuned two days later with a truck.

*****

"Mr. King?" Margaret asked when she opened the door to find a circus on her front porch.

"Yes, ma'am. I'm sorry but the bank has foreclosed on the house, furnishings and the car," the insurance man informed. The men behind him barged in and got to work.

"What are they doing, mama? Who are these people?" young prince moaned when men spread throughout the house, seizing anything of value. His mother clutched her purse tightly since it contained the life savings she found.

"Don't worry. It's fine," Margaret said but she was wrong. It was not nor would it be fine. In fact, life would never be fine again. The corrupt insurance company conspired with the corrupt sheriff's department and put the family out of their home. "Go get your clothes. Hurry!"

Prince took off and loaded his modest clothes, and prized possessions. He grabbed his beloved books since he was an avid reader. The boy spent most of his free time in books, from the bible to his favorite vampire books. He was now an expert in both topics. His mother did the same and barely retrieved the money her husband stashed before her bedroom filled with treasure hunters, looking for valuables and caches of cash.

"Where we going, mama?" he whined when she rushed him out of the back door as if they were the ones stealing. She had come to the country illegally, so she couldn't put up a fight for the house and property.

"I'm not su—" she was beginning to say but the appearance of a sheriff deputy changed the answer still in her throat.

"Ma'am, I need you two to come with me," he stated and held his arm up to guide them towards his vehicle. He didn't pull his gun or cuffs, but they were still under arrest.

"Don't say anything, you hear?" Margaret told her son softly as they were seated in the back seat. His mouth opened anyway, so she repeated herself a little louder.

"Listen to your mama now, boy," the redneck offered over his shoulder. He wouldn't mind if the boy got out of line so he could beat him right back in line. "You two are going to immigration. You can't sneak into our country and get away with it. One day someone needs to build a wall to keep you people out!"

"We're from Haiti, not Mexico!" Margaret spat. It was her only defense because she was still here illegally.

"I was born h—" Prince began but once again was cut off. This time a hard slap helped get the point across. Prince huffed, puffed and pouted but remained quiet until they reached a holding cell down at the immigration office.

"I'm sorry, my dear son. These people are going to deport me. You were born here, yes, but you can not live on your own," she explained, while rubbing the spot where her slap touched.

Prince understood but his mind shot between Sister Clara's big brown legs. The older widow begged him to move in with her after she rode him to the first orgasm of her life. He did in twenty minutes what her husband of twenty years couldn't. He could live there, but he wouldn't leave his mother.

"I understand mother," he said and lifted his chin. He was the man of the house now, even though men were rummaging through the house stealing and confiscating anything they could find. "What about the house? What about daddy?"

"Nothing I can do about either," she said and attempted to lift her chin as well. It was too heavy with grief to raise and the tears began to stream. Her husband paid his insurance premiums faithfully and they denied his claim. Instead of a dignified burial, he would be placed in a cardboard box and left to rot in a shallow grave. Then the house he was so proud of was stolen from under him. The white folks hated that he was able to afford to be their neighbors.

They knew once one black family moved in, many more would come. They were right, too, because in a few years, the whole neighborhood would be black. White flight began as the whites took flight and the neighborhood turned into the hood. What goes around would come back around when they came back fifty years later and reclaimed the area. High taxes and home prices forced the black families right back out again.

"You come back when you're older, stronger and take back what they took from us. Promise! Swear!" Margaret insisted. His head began to nod with an angry scowl on his handsome face.

"I'm going to take it and more. I'm going to take everything they love," Prince vowed. He felt a new emotion seep through his soul rage.

CHAPTER 2

After a kangaroo court of an immigration hearing, Margaret and Prince were officially deported to Haiti. Margaret feared how her son would deal with his new life in a new country. She would get her answer shortly since the long ride by ship was over.

"Wow!" Martin proclaimed when he got a glimpse of his new land. It was also where he got his new name when he read the battered sign announcing, "Port a Prince."

"I know. I'm sorry, baby," Margaret whined since she knew his wasn't a "wow'"of awe, but one of shock instead.

The busy Port of Prince, Haiti seemed to move a mile a minute. Shifty eyes scanned the area in search of prey and corruption hung in the air like Beijing smog. Robbers roamed and hookers hooked, both in search of the same thing. Both would eagerly slit their throats for a few dollars.

"Taxi?" a man called out and beckoned for them to come near. Prince took a step towards his car until his mother pulled him back. She spit a malicious yet melodic tirade in the man's direction in French that made him slink away.

Prince cocked his head curiously at his mother and awaited an explanation to the event.

"Him, a robber? He 'ah take us to the alley and take our 'tings," she spelled out. He noticed her English had taken a turn for the worse once they landed. She hadn't gotten to speak her native French in years, but it came back in an instant. She also hardened right in front of his eyes like Lot's wife when she stayed behind. The woman was soft and girly in their Atlanta home. Now she was as rough as a mechanic's hands.

Margaret hailed an official taxi to a small village on the outskirts of town. Most of the houses were handmade of sticks and stones wouldn't stand up to a huff and puff from the big bad wolf. Some were even worse, made from discarded pieces of wood or corrugated metal. They were hot enough in the brutal summers to bake bread without an oven.

Prince breathed a sigh of relief when they pulled to a stop in front of a solid wooden house. It was shanty compared to the house they just left, but a mansion next to some of the other houses. His mother was careful not to let the driver see her stash of cash as she paid him. She waited and counted her change before budging from the backseat. Then waited again until her son removed all of their bags before relinquishing her seat. Many a tourist have made the mistake of stepping out of a cab and then pulling their bags out, only to have the driver pull away immediately and take all of their possessions. Haiti is a third world country on a good day. On a bad one, it's far, far worse.

Margaret spit something in rapid fire French over her shoulder as she stomped towards the house. Prince didn't know the language but knew the tone, so he stayed put and waited for her to come back. In the meanwhile, he let his eyes roam the village and it's inhabitants.

"Wow," he repeated as the abject poverty sank in. He knew there were better places in Atlanta than where he lived and he knew there were worse. This was even worse than their worst.

Dirty, barefoot children scrounged in garbage piles in search of scraps of meat, despite abundant fruits hanging from the trees. Meat didn't grow on trees, so they searched the garbage for bones or marrow. A beautiful girl around his age stepped out of a shanty and shed her tiny dress. Her bronze skin had a brilliant sheen from sweat of the afternoon heat. He watched as she bathed from a bucket right there on the side of her house. His piercing gaze burned her skin and caused her to look up. She was as mesmerized by the newcomer as he was by her nakedness.

"Let the girl bathe in peace. The only privacy she has is in you not looking," Margaret advised as she came back outside. "Come, meet your family."

"Okay, can I—" Prince began to ask but she left him alone with all the bags. He pulled a juggling act and loaded them on his arms and went inside.

An older woman rushed and gushed over him when he stepped inside. He didn't understand her praise, so he turned to his mother for help. She inspected the tall boy as if she planned to buy him and cook him for dinner.

"She is your grandmother. She says you are very handsome!" Margaret spelled out proudly. Once the old lady had her fill, she showed them to the room they would share. His mother translated most of what she said. Not all since some rapid fire paragraphs might only get a sentence in translation. Once they were settled in, both took a long nap to recover from the long journey.

"Mph," Prince groaned when his full bladder nudged him awake from the inside. He searched in vain for a bathroom before remembering the outhouse, outside of the house.

Prince was no punk but still paused in trepidation when he opened the back door. He had never seen a dark as dark as this night was, nor the sounds of the nocturnal creatures that ruled the night. The fear of peeing his pants outweighed the fear of the unknown, so he stepped outside and went to relieve himself.

"Ugh!" he grunted when he stepped inside of the small outhouse. It was a small wooden structure built over a deep hole in the ground. It was overdue to be filled in with dirt from the new hole and moved. He held his breath as he emptied his bladder, then rushed back inside.

*****

"Shoot!" Prince complained when he awoke the next morning. Not just because of the stifling heat, but because he had to go back out to the outhouse.

"Good morning, my dear," Margaret greeted when she came in from bathing. Haiti required several baths each day.

"I miss our bathroom," he pouted and rolled out the bed.

"I'm sorry," she apologized once again. She was used to the hard life here but hated it for him. "I filled the bucket for you to bathe. Hurry so you can come eat."

"Okay, mama," Prince relented since she was as much a victim as he was. He manned up and went outside to handle his business. He held his breath and peed as hard as he could to get out of the hot box.

He was relieved to see the bathing bucket was in the back of the house so he could have some privacy. He would need it too since the memory of the girl from yesterday made him rise and quiver. No one wants to walk around with a hard dick, so he devised a plan to make it soft again. He shot a glance in each direction and took matters into his own hand.

"Mmm," Prince moaned as he began to stroke himself. He had a mental ménage as he switched between memories of Sister Clara from the choir and the exotic beauty from yesterday. His eyes closed and knees bent when it got good to him.

"Shit!" Prince grunted when he reached his peak and began to spew his seeds safely on the ground below. It was a good one until he looked up and saw his confused grandmother staring back. She muttered something in French and stepped back inside.

His mind tried to recall the way back to the airport. It would be a long walk but better than facing the old woman again after that. In the end, he still couldn't leave his mother, so he finished bathing and stepped inside. He could only hope the old lady didn't tell his mother.

"Martin!" Margaret shrieked when he came inside, and dashed those hopes on the rocks. His grandmother was still snitching on him in the foreign language. He knew what she was saying since she imitated his hand movements.

"No, I wasn't!" he shot back since she couldn't understand him. They argued back and forth in different languages while Margaret looked to and fro like a tennis match.

"You two are too much!" Margaret laughed. She knew her son becoming a man and was glad he took care of it himself instead of one of the women around here. She knew better than most that these women were dangerous. She would know since she was one of them.

"What about school?" Prince asked once his grandmother calmed down. She was still twisting her lip at him but stopped griping.

Margaret spit some rapid fire French, knowing he wouldn't understand.

"Excuse me, ma'am?"

"This is school until you learn the language. You must learn the language," she insisted. Prince immediately tuned in and learned every word spoken in his presence.

Within a week, he was able to have a basic conversation in his adopted language. He would need it for whenever he ran into the girl from across the street again. They saw each other and stared a few times but had yet to meet face to face.

"Go get a can of milk, eggs..." Prince's grandmother said slowly as he nodded along. She made sure to put the money on the table instead of his hand since she saw what he does with his hands. The money came from his mother who had been paying for everything since they arrived. Margaret never said no, and the money was dwindling quickly.

"And stay away from that girl. She 'ah trouble ya know," Margaret warned. She didn't know the child but remembered her mother from growing up. She knew she was trouble because they were best friends at one point.

"Yes," he replied in French. It was his first lie in his new language, because he couldn't wait to see her again.

Prince was always amazed at the sights and sounds of the village. It was a far cry from the busy capital but busy nonetheless. The strange smells and sounds of the people fascinated him. He was so fascinated, he walked right into the girl when he entered the store.

She spun and launched into a profanity-laced tirade he could understand since, come to find out, his grandmother cursed a lot. The girl retracted the venom and softened at the sight of the handsome newcomer. She had been waiting on this moment

",Bonjour" she sang, smiled, and batted her almond shaped eyes. Prince just blinked in her glaring beauty. She was something from across the street but she was something else up close.

Her bronze skin shone and glistened and her firm breasts pressed against the thin fabric of her dress. Luckily, they stood firm on their own since she couldn't afford braziers. Or shoes for that matter, revealing feet made rough by the miles she put on them everyday.

"Bonjour?" she repeated and laughed at him being stuck. She knew she was pretty but never got a reaction like that before. Grown men may glare and stare but were too afraid of her grandmother to approach.

"Bonjour," he apologized and got himself together. She was just as taken with him in person as he was of her.

"Antoinette," she explained and pointed at herself.

"Prince," Prince offered and pointed at himself, as well. His foreign accent sank in and moistened her panties in an instant. Most of the inhabitants dreamed of the beautiful foreigner who would swoop in and carry them away from the misery and poverty of the island. She had saved her cherry for a rainy day and felt storm clouds gathering in her panties.

"America?" she asked hopefully. It was most Haitians first choice, followed closely by anywhere but here.

"America," he replied and nodded. The two were inseparable from that moment on.

Prince realized fairly quickly that the girl intended to hold on to her virginity but that didn't stop them from spending most of most days together. He was virtually fluent in French in a month's time. The downside was his grandmother catching him masturbating a few more times.

*****

"Going back with that girl?" Margaret asked when she saw her son brushing his hair. She now spoke to him exclusively in French.

"Yes," he said and waited for her tirade about the girl's mother. He gleamed from her many rants that they once shared a man. Antoinette's mother won the battle and left her scorned.

Today's rant had a little extra on it because Margaret had reached the end of her money. The last of the food was cooking in the pot and something had to give. She knew her son wasn't cut out for the hard labor of the farms nor would she subject him to that brutal work. He was only here because of her, so she tried to spare him of the ugly.

Ugly spares no one and plenty was on it's ugly way to rear it's ugly head. Her attitude was ugly because she had ugly plans for the evening.

He insisted they weren't having sex when her talk turned to unwanted grandchildren. She heard the truth and angst in his tone and changed speed.

Antoinette was nothing like her mother and took after the churchgoing grandmother who took care of her. She didn't wear much clothing because they were poor and it was dreadfully hot. Still, she was chaste and saving herself for marriage one day.

"Well, I have to go in to the city tonight. I want you to stay here and take care of your grandmother," Margaret said. He heard her tone as well and cancelled the plans he had with Antoinette. They usually sat by the river to catch fish for her dinner and watch the sunset together. She would have to watch it without him because he would not leave the sick old lady alone.

Now it was his turn to watch his mother get gussied up for a night in the city. Prince felt sad at the notion of her getting pretty for some man. That would have been bad since his father died only six months ago. The truth, however, was far worse than her going on a date. She was going on as many dates as she could before the sun rose.

CHAPTER 3

"Are you coming?" Antoinette asked when Prince stepped out to greet her.

"I can't. My mother went to town. I have to watch my grandmother," he pouted. His pout was nothing compared to hers. Hers almost got that old lady left by herself.

"That's ok," she said in the English he had taught her and smiled. She switched back to French and reminded him, "We have forever!"

"Forever," he agreed and smiled to match hers. Antoinette shot a glance in each direction to make sure the coast was clear. It wasn't, but she didn't see the group of local boys in the cut when she leaned up and kissed his full lips. The instant erection from the kiss almost got the old lady left once more. So did the jiggling ass cheeks under the thin dress as she skipped happily away. The kiss had her as giddy as he was hard, but the guys glared in jealous rage.

The group of teens scowled as they watched the beautiful girl they watched and waited to bloom and blossom only for the poor American to get her. It was bad enough that he lived in the best house in the village but now he took the prettiest girl. The boys waited until Prince closed the door before following behind Antoinette.

"She is resting, so stay close. She will need her medicine when she wakes up," Margaret explained and kissed her son's face.

"Yes, mother," Prince nodded and watched her get into the waiting car. There wasn't much to do, so he went to read the vampire book he'd read several times before.

"Bonjour," the driver greeted and reached back to fondle Margaret's legs. He'd been wanting to do that for quite some time, but her large son was always with her. Now she could either let him or stop him.

"Bonjour," she greeted and spread her firm legs to get him closer to the promise land. Any hooker worth her salt knows the promise of pussy is more valuable than the pussy itself. Any pussy, no matter how tight, wet, or hot, loses some of its value once it's been conquered.

He got his feel on the whole ride into the busy capital. Once he realized her final destination, he regretted not pulling over and fucking her on the side of the road. The only Haitian women who frequented this particular bar favored by foreigners, supplied the good Haitian pussy favored by foreigners. He still had the audacity to request full fare when he pulled to a stop in front of the Port a Prince lounge.

"Here you are," Margaret said as she placed exactly half of the agreed upon price into his hand.

"Where is the rest?" he asked as his face twisted in confusion.

"On your fingers," she reminded and hopped out of his car. He watched her round ass walk away while sucking the sweet nectar she left on his fingers.

*****

"Where is your American boyfriend?" the leader of the pack asked Antoinette when they came upon her at the riverbank.

"None of your business, Jon Paul!" Antoinette shot back and fiddled with her makeshift fishing pole when she felt a nibble.

"Well, this is my business," he declared and grabbed one of her breast. He had copped feels before but this time she was so shocked, she whirled around and slapped his face.

The crack of the slap reverberated in the thin, country air as everyone froze to figure out what happened and more importantly what would happen next. John Paul reeled and slapped her so hard, she hit the ground. Her legs flew open when she landed and he wasted no time in his next move.

"John Paul?" one of his friends asked when he pounced between her legs. The rip of her frail panties sent the girl into a panic. She flailed her arms and slapped at his face as he struggled to remove his pants.

"Hold her arms!" he demanded and his flunkies rushed to carry out the command.

Antoinette fought valiantly but was no match for the five guys, one on each limb and one spitting on her labia to ease his entry. She let out a shrill scream when he forcefully and rudely penetrated her. He clamped a hand over her mouth and began to thrust his hips. The excitement and tightness limited his thrust to a few before he grunted and ejaculated inside of her. He slumped over ready for a nap but his friends wanted in as well literally, taking turns from what did not belong to them. She had vowed it to Prince but didn't get to keep it. He was all she thought about as the five guys ravaged her virginity. It was her prized possession and they were laughing it up, while taking it away. Prince would never want her now. Not after she turned him down and made him wait.

Jon Paul climbed on board once again when his turn came back around. The night was young so they all had plenty turns coming.

*****

Margaret fought back tears when she entered the same bar she sold herself in when she was young. It was a means to an end and in the end, she made it all the way to America. She had come full circle and ended right back where she started from.

"You were right, mother," she muttered to herself. Oddly, her mother had no qualms about her renting herself to the foreigners since it allowed her to build her house. There wasn't any work on the island and selling pussy isn't work but still paid the bills. She had a fit when Margaret told her she was moving to America with a man.

The old place looked exactly the same except the girls seemed younger. She remembered being young herself when she first began working the bar. Back when a smooth, yet brutal pimp named Claude seduced, then pimped her. She felt his presence and scanned the dimly lit room. There he was on his usual roost staring back from behind a swirl of cigarette smoke. This was his domain. so there was no use in trying to ignore him. She lifted her head and marched over to him.

"Bonjour," Margaret sighed and nodded in defeat. Claude had aged well and was just as handsome and arrogant as ever. Most of his women left in death, not by choice.

"You're late," he said smugly as he looked at the fancy gold watch that came courtesy of one of his own clients. "How long has it been?"

"Twenty years," she answered quickly since it was almost to the day. "Same arrangement?"

"Maybe. Perhaps I take sixty percent. A fine for leaving me all alone," Claude offered.

"Alone?" she scoffed and looked around at all the girls and women selling themselves on his behalf. He was generous enough to let them keep half of what they earned. He decided to tax Margaret an extra ten percent for breaking his heart. "Claude, you are never alone."

"No, but I will get a taste, for old times sake," he said and stood. He wished he had the time to take her for a spin now but paying customers awaited. Come to find out, while the

41

foreign men slinked into bars and alleys in search of some strange pussy, their women stayed back in the hotel and placed orders for some strange dick.

"Of course you will. And it will cost you that ten percent," she said to his back. Claude chuckled and nodded as he walked away to sleep with a pasty white lady whose husband was upstairs sleeping with one of his girls.

Margaret didn't wait long before being selected by a vacationer from Europe.

"Bonjour," he said as he read off a card. The bellhop at the hotel wrote down a few crucial sayings for him so he could navigate the nightlife.

"Bonjour," Margaret replied and wondered if his little card contained the words for what he was after. It did and he carefully asked for some pussy in broken pieces of French. His money was whole so she put her arm in his and left the bar.

*****

"What now?" one of the boys asked their leader once they all took several turns in Antoinette.

Jon Paul looked down at the traumatized girl staring up with empty eyes. He knew he went too far but there was no way back. Never in the history of rape has a woman been unraped. He didn't have the guts to say it out loud, so he kneeled down and placed his hands around her neck.

Antoinette leaned her head back and didn't resist. He had stolen her chastity so why not take her life. Dying with dignity beat living with shame. She would have to see these boys every day of her life. They would certainly rape her again. Probably every day. She began to fade away as her oxygen supply was cut off. She passed out, then passed on.

No one spoke on the way back to the village. None would ever speak of it again out of shame. There was no police department or CSI to collect the gobs of DNA they left inside of her. The Bible was the law of the land, so an eye for an eye was the only justice. If they were found out, the men of the village, including their own fathers, would certainly kill them.

Meanwhile, Prince had to pour medicine in his grandmother's mouth since she wouldn't wake up. He then sat on the porch with a book to enjoy the gentle breeze once the sun set. Plus, keep an eye out for his mother or Antoinette when they returned.

He watched the pack of boys emerge from the path that led to the river. They all glanced over, then abruptly cut their eyes away when they saw him looking back. He knew then that something was wrong, just not how wrong.

Antoinette's grandmother came out an hour later and looked over at Prince to see if Antoinette was over there. They locked eyes for a moment before she went back inside.

The night fell and the cool air rocked Prince to sleep right there on the porch. Margaret returned just before dawn but decided not to wake him. Not just yet anyway and stepped into the room to undress. She filled a hot water bottle with lukewarm water and stepped out into the backyard. She had a good night and made good money, but she was so full of semen she squished when she walked. She flushed her insides out, then washed the outside and went back inside.

Claude was happy to have one of his best earners back and she didn't disappoint. Time had changed and the new crop of young girls were transient and unpredictable. She checked in with him before leaving and gave up half of her earnings in exchange for a ride home and reservations for tomorrow night.

"Mama?" Margaret called softly as she poked her head in to check on her mother. There was no reply, so she came closer. She was pleased to see her son had given her her medicine. She leaned in and planted a kiss on the woman's cheek, and felt the cold stiffness of death. Nothing could be done now, so she went into her room and went to bed.

CHAPTER 4

Prince awoke with the crowing of a rooster. He knew by now that dawn was minutes away. It was the cue for the vampire in his latest book to seek cover from the deadly daylight.

An attitude began to form when he realized his mother hadn't returned from her night out. He knew that meant she had sex with some man, spreading a scowl on his face. It dissipated upon entering the room they shared as he found her sleeping hard and snoring lightly.

He waited until the sun rose a little before going to check on Antoinette since she hadn't checked on him when she returned. Her grandmother was already standing on her porch looking to and fro, so he knew she hadn't returned.

"Bonjour," the old lady called and waved frantically as she came over. "Is Antoinette here?"

"Bonjour, no?" he asked and joined her panic. "She was going to the bank. To fish."

"She hasn't come home. Go look for her!" she insisted and pulled him from his door. He didn't like to leave without telling his mother but didn't have much of a choice.

"Yes," he agreed and took off. Antoinette loved to nap on the bank during the day, but the animals came out at night to feed. He rushed through the Haitian jungle to collect his girl and hurry back before Margaret awoke.

"Antoinette! Your grandmother is looking for you!" he called as he neared their favorite spot. He wasn't sure to be relieved or not when he didn't see her where he knew she would be. It was short-lived when he saw her tattered dress on the ground. That must have meant she took a dip, so he rushed over to catch a glimpse of her emerging from the river. If her dress were here then she would be naked. His excitement was dashed when he saw her shredded panties. A scan of the rivers edge provided the worst possible outcome. There was what remained of Antoinette partially eaten and partially submerged in the water.

Wild animals had eaten their fill before a small cayman attempted to take the rest into the river. Prince pulled her from the water to take her home. The best he could do was cover part of her with her dress and carried her away.

Antoinette's grandmother was still waiting outside when he returned. She perked up for a moment when he saw them, until he drew nearer and she saw her condition. The old lady let out a howl that brought the neighbors to their doors and windows, including his mother.

"Martin!" Margaret yelled when she saw her son involved in whatever was going on. He gently placed the battered body on the ground in front of her grandmother.

"I found her like this," he explained to his worried mother. She grew up here and knew the eye for an eye code they lived by. She also knew her son would die by it, if they thought he hurt the girl.

Jon Paul and friends gathered at a safe distance and watched the proceedings. The village elder made his way over to investigate what was going on. Prince was the newcomer and suspicion immediately fell on him. Antoinette's grandmother was able to vouch for him since she knew he was home and she was not..

"Go inside!" Margaret demanded when the crowd began to grow. Prince heard the news of his grandmother over his shoulder as he went inside. He rushed into her room and saw the sheet was pulled over her head. For the second time in less than a year, he had lost another loved one. The ugly of life was just getting started.

Prince eased to the window and listened to the crowd speculation about who killed the girl. He wanted to step out and let them know about the boys but knew it was his word against theirs. Margaret was able to calm them with the news of her own mother's death. She was beloved to all and granted a reprieve to bury their dead.

"What are they saying mother?" he asked when she returned.

"You will not be safe here! Not until I can find out what really happened. Pack your things," she insisted.

47

"Where am I going?" he asked and got yelled at because Margaret had no idea where he was going. She just knew he had to leave here. Prince went to pack his belongings and books once more while his mother sneaked down to the neighbor who drove her to town.

"What do you want?" the man's wife spat when she answered the door. The last thing she wanted was her husband spending time with the pretty woman.

"To hire your husband to drive me again. Just like he did yesterday that put meat in your pot," she reminded. The woman had to admit swallowing meat tasted better than swallowing pride, so she called for her husband.

"Marquis! The woman needs another ride!" she said and thought about how to cook the chicken she would buy.

"Now?" Marquis asked when he came out and saw Margaret. He already agreed to be her ride to town each evening, but it was still morning.

"Yes now, and later. I will pay extra," she vowed and sealed the deal. "Just meet me in front of my house in ten minutes."

The wife knew something was wrong but it had been months since she had a whole chicken in her clutches. Whatever it was would have to wait until after she fed her family.

"I'm packed, mama. What about grandmother?" Prince asked. He knew it was the custom of the country to bury their dead as

48

soon as possible. There were no mortuaries nor embalming in those days and bodies get ripe quickly in the heat.

"I will take care of her. You must go!" she repeated. They took his meager belongings to the front door and waited for Marquis to pull up. There were people out so they would be spotted, but not stopped. Several eyes watched Marquis pull to a squeaky stop in front of the house. They saw the mother and son rushed out and get in. He pulled away before anyone could open their mouth, but the jury had returned and pronounced Prince guilty.

Prince wanted to ask where they were going but held his tongue when he saw the sign bearing his name, Port a Prince. The turn-by-turn directions she gave the driver said she knew exactly where she was going. The ride ended in front of a small but lavish bungalow surrounded by a barbwire fence.

"Wait here!" Margaret demanded to both as she hopped out and marched towards the fence. The watch man popped up out of nowhere and met her.

"Who you looking for?" he demanded and squinted at the woman.

"This is Claude's house, so I must be looking for Claude!" she shot back. That set off a back and forth debate that eventually got Claude out of bed to see what all the fuss was about.

"Margaret?" he asked as in, what are you doing here, since he had just dropped her off. He would have brought her here but had nothing left after the large woman he bedded last night. He left it all inside of his customers. Customers like her, along with contributions by a hundred whores allowed him to build the mini palace in the heart of the city.

"I need to speak with you. Tell him to get out of my way!" she demanded. Claude fussed and the watchman stepped aside and opened the gate. Claude squinted at the boy and driver sitting in the car. He assumed whatever was so urgent had something to do with him, so he held his questions until she finished.

"How can I help you?" he asked. Of course he needed to know so he could know how much to charge her. He mentally started at ten percent and was ready to raise the amount the moment she opened her mouth.

"My son needs to stay here! There is trouble in the village," she explained without explaining what kind of trouble. She guessed correctly that he would turn her away if he knew the boy could be wanted for murder.

"I am a pimp, not a nanny," he laughed and took a sip of whiskey to prove it.

"He's not a baby. He can help out around here. He's smarter than that dummy you have working your gate," she offered then sealed the deal with, "And he is American!"

"American?" Claude practically shouted and hopped to his feet. "How old is he?"

50

"Seventeen," she said, adding a few months since his birthday was soon.

"Bring him," he said eagerly and she took off just as eagerly. Margaret shot the watchman a side eye like his days were numbered as she went to retrieve her son.

"Wait for me," she told Marquis as she let Prince out. He grabbed his bags and fell in step behind her.

Claude was skeptical until Margaret returned with a goldmine in tow. Prince looked more like a man than a boy and his customers of both sexes would love him. He managed to contain his excitement and pretended not to be impressed.

"Martin, this is Claude. I need you to listen to him. I'll be back in a few days," she said and turned to leave before Claude could shut her down.

"This will cost you twenty percent!" he called after her. She waved her hand and stepped from the house. Claude turned to Prince and inspected him once again. He spoke perfect English and asked "America?"

"America. Atlanta, Georgia," Prince said proudly. It was the first time he got to speak English since he arrived. Little did he know it wouldn't be his last.

CHAPTER 5

"You must not tell anyone where we took my son! Do you understand?" Margaret demanded when she returned to the car. "If they ask, tell them we took him to the port. He boarded a boat back to America!"

"What is going on?" Marquis asked. He saw the commotion in the village this morning but had yet to get the details. Margaret debated on telling him but knew he would find out as soon as they returned. It was better he hear her version before anything else.

"Antoinette was killed this morning. My son was in the house all night with his grandmother. She was sick. She died, as well," she explained. She left out the part of the rumors of Martin being involved.

"Mademoiselle!" he mourned and crossed his catholic heart. The religious moment passed a moment later when he pulled to the side of the road. "I will not tell a soul, but..."

"I see," Margaret said once she translated his request. She hiked her dress enough to remove her panties and turned around.

Her head was out of the passenger window when she got on her hands and knees in the front seat. Marquis scrambled to free his erection and rushed it inside of her. Margaret was a professional and moaned like he was the best lover in the world. The excitement caused him to climax quickly but he hung in there and went for seconds. This time took a lot longer since he intended to get his money's worth. It took some doing but he managed to maneuver her onto her back so he could fuck her face to face, looking down at her pretty face as he finally made love to her did the trick.

Marquis grunted and filled her with yet another serving of semen. There would be plenty more since she still planned to work tonight. It would be business as usual until things calmed down and her son could come home.

"You cannot go to sleep in it," she warned when he slumped on top of her and didn't move.

"I know," Marquis said sadly and begrudgingly removed himself from her self. He looked down at her vagina and sighed like he would miss it. Margaret fixed her clothes and sat up straight for the rest of the ride home. Her first stop was to Franco, the village elder so she could bury her mother.

"Where is the boy?" the man asked as soon as she was let inside.

"Safe," was all he was getting out of her. "Mademoiselle has passed away. We need to bury her."

"We will bury her, then I must talk with your son. The boys tell me he was with her last night,"

"I see," she nodded. Two of the boys were his great grandsons, so it wouldn't be much of a talk. Once her mother was safely in the ground, she would make her escape, as well. There were no more reasons for her to stay without her family.

*****

The mood was doubly tense at the double funeral. The faces displayed more malice than mourning. Putting the young girl in the ground created more beef than grief. All eyes were on Margaret since she brought this monster to their community.

Graves had to be dug extra deep so that the animals wouldn't dig them up. This was learned the hard way after dogs were seen with parts of their dearly departed. The same boys who caused the need for one of the holes helped dig the holes. Margaret counted three holes and knew one was for her son.

One of the many hats worn by Franco was the preacher. He gave a two beautiful sermons for the beautiful souls laying in the boxes. He was also the sheriff, judge, jury and sometimes executioner, when needed. The somber funerals wrapped up and families walked back to their homes.

Margaret walked slowly back to her house so she wouldn't draw any unnecessary attention. She couldn't have drawn any more attention than she had if she set herself on fire and walked on her hands. All eyes had been on her during the funerals and all eyes were on here as she made her way home. It was time for her to pack and leave, as well. Now that she was selling herself, she could easily make enough money to find a place in town for her and her son. If she made it out that is.

"Marquis, Franco wants to speak with you," a man said as the village driver slinked back to his house.

"Moi?" he asked as if another Marquis was standing there. The man didn't answer the silly question and led the way to see the elder.

"Come in," Franco barked to the knock on his door. In walked the two men and joined the others inside. Marquis knew he was in trouble when he saw all the angry faces.

"Bonjour?" he asked and looked around. The elder let him fester for almost a full minute before speaking.

"Where did you take the boy?" he wanted to know. Not 'if' but where. Marquis thought about Margaret and the honey pot between her legs for a split second and lied. He wanted some more as soon and as often as possible so he repeated what he was told.

"To the port. She put him on a ship back to America," he answered quickly. Perhaps not quick enough, because a nod of the elder's head sent a machete speeding his way. The super sharp blade knocked his arm off so smoothly, he didn't know what had happened. He looked curiously at the familiar looking body part below until an arch of blood skeeting from his shoulder stole his attention.

"I swear! I swear that is where I took him!" he vowed. He misunderstood the punishment thinking it was due to his lie. He stuck to his story since he could still make love to Margaret with one arm.

"That boy killed one of our own and you helped him get away," Franco spat and nodded once more. This nod sent a flurry of blades that shredded the man on the spot. The village elder had just inherited a vehicle. "Bring the mother to me."

"We're going to need another hole," a man said as he left to carryout the order.

"Shit!" Margaret fussed when she heard her front door open without knocking. Only two people had the right to do that. One was freshly buried and the other safely hidden in the city. She grabbed her own cutlass and rushed out to face the intruder.

"Aaaaah!" Margaret screamed with the machete raised over her head. She may go out but not without a fight. The man was unarmed since he was just on a mission to bring her back. Figuratively at first, but when he raised his arm to deflect the blow, he was literally unarmed. Her banshee scream was nothing compared to the howl he let out when he saw his arm on the ground. He reached for it with the other hand and lost that one, too. She knew his screams would be heard and answered, so she grabbed one of her bags and hit the door.

"There she is!" one of the boys who started this avalanche of grief and murder yelled and pointed as Margaret ran. She knew she couldn't outrun the village but wasn't going to sit around and wait to be killed. Nor would she ever give up her son, so she made a run for it.

The men and boys quickly caught up with her and surrounded her. She lunged and took swipes with her cutlass but the men didn't fight back. They just used their own blades and sticks to block her blows until the elder arrived.

The women of the village formed an outer circle and hissed, while raising sticks and kitchen knives. Antoinette's grandmother got caught in the mob mentality as well, even though she knew the boy had nothing to do with her death. She was dead nonetheless and blood requires blood to be avenged. This village had no idea how much blood would one day be lost.

"You should not have sent him back to America," Franco said softly. He nodded even softer and set off a massacre.

Once again, Margaret didn't go down without a fight. She screamed as loud as she could and tried to take them all with her. She managed to score a few good wounds on her attackers before she fell under the blades and clubs. Once she was as good as dead, the women moved in and finished her off with their brooms, sticks and paring knives. Even Sophia stuck the corpse once or twice but only because she had to. She too worked for Claude and would report what happened when she went in to town. For now, she joined the women and rummaged through her bag. The elder claimed the wooden house and moved in.

Things calmed down soon after both bodies were drug into the jungle to feed the animals, an eerie calm that comes before the storm. A storm was coming, too. It was a few years away but promised to wipe this village off the face of the earth.

CHAPTER 6

"So, what do you like to do in America?" Claude asked when Prince won the staring contest. He had hoped to intimidate the teen by glaring at him since his mother left. It didn't work because Prince just stared right back.

"School," he answered quickly and countered with a question of his own, now that they were talking. "When is my mother coming back?"

"Later. Do you have a girlfriend? Do you like girls?" the man asked to see which way to sell the boy. He had both male and female clients who would love the handsome teen.

"No. Yes," he shot back and paused, while Claude matched the answers with his questions. "I had a girlfriend but she died. The boys killed her."

Claude listened and heard the reason why he was here. His first thought was to run to his car and rush out to the village. He knew first hand how primitive they could be. Even now in the year 1963, they behaved like cavemen. He could only hope Margaret made it out safely.

"Will your guest join you for supper, Monsieur Claude?" the elderly cook asked as she finished cooking dinner. There was plenty of food, so she wanted to know how many plates to make.

"Yes," he said since he knew Prince would be there for many meals.

Once supper was served, it would be time for the magic show to begin. No rabbits would be pulled from hats or women sawed in half, but there would be plenty of tricks performed.

"Is my mother coming now?" Prince asked when the meal was done. He hoped she was staying here with them instead of taking him back to the village. With Antoinette and his grandmother gone, there was nothing for him there.

Not to mention the food was good and the bathroom was inside. He couldn't wait to flush the toilet just for old times sake. A shower instead of bathing out of a bucket would also be nice.

He liked it here already, but liked it even more when Sophia arrived. He'd seen her several times in the village but was warned to stay away from her. Not that he cared since he and Antoinette were together all the time.

"Bonjour Claude, they—" Sophia began, excitedly then stopped abruptly when she saw Prince was present. The look on her face told Prince it was bad, but worse than he could imagine.

"Come," Claude directed and led her into his bedroom. He closed the door behind them so they could speak in privacy. "What?"

"They killed her. Margaret. Killed her dead," she relayed, leaving out getting a few stabs in herself.

"Wow," he muttered and sank down to his bed. He crossed his heart once more and silently contemplated his next move. He had plans for the boy and Margaret would have certainly objected. That obstacle was gone, but he had to tread carefully. The humane thing to do would be to inform the boy, but Claude was far from humane. In fact, he was barely human.

"Are you going to tell the boy?" Sophia asked when she saw the wheels were turning in his head.

"Yes, just not yet. Here's what I want you to do..." he decided and laid out his plans. Sophia smiled wickedly partly because she was wicked but also because she liked his wicked plan.

Claude showered and dressed for the night on the town. He had no appointments of his own for the night, so he would go to his bar and manage the girls. Prince looked up when they emerged from the bedroom. He expected to be briefed on whatever was going on, but Claude had other plans.

"I must handle business. Sophia will stay here with you," he said and left before the boy could question him. Sophia had been briefed on how to answer all of his questions until he returned.

"Where is my mother? Did you see her?" Prince asked as soon as he and Sophia were alone.

"Resting. It is a very hard time in the village right now. Give her a few days," she said and poured two drinks. Prince accepted his to be polite even though he did not drink.

"Oh," he said and sat the glass on the glass table.

"Don't be rude," Sophia giggled and took a sip of her whiskey. Prince was raised not to be rude, so he took a sip as well.

"Ugh!" Prince reeled form the bitter liquor. Sophia laughed out loud at the grimace the strong drink put on his face. It stung on its own, then again when she tossed back her glass with a straight face. Not to be out done, he tilted his head and drained his own glass. This time he handled the burn and kept his face straight.

"That's more like it!" she cheered and poured another round. This time she filled both glasses to the rim. Prince didn't want anymore but didn't want to get laughed at again either. The next round, they both sipped their drinks and struck up conversation.

"Tell me about America! How is it?" Sophia asked with stars in her eyes. She had heard the rivers were honey and the streets lined with gold. Only from other people who'd never been to America themselves.

"Nothing like this," he admitted. They were by no means rich in America but now poverty had a new perspective. The city was ten steps ahead of the village but ten years behind home in America.

"I would like to go one day," she admitted wistfully. She hadn't yet been born when a sailor took Margaret away but heard tales of it growing up. The dream of every working girl was to be carted off to America or Canada or England.

"I'm going back when I'm older. I was born there, so I'm allowed," he said to her delight.

"Will you take me?" she pleaded. She stood and stepped out of the tiny dress she wore and asked again. "Please!"

"I—" Prince began before being cut off by her nudity. Sophia realized she had him hooked and moved in to reel him in.

She sashayed over and knelt before him. Prince looked down and watched curiously as she removed the rock hard erection from his pants. He blinked in disbelief as he disappeared into her mouth and down her throat. Sister Clara gave it up from the front, side and back but never went down on him. This was a first and felt fantastic.

The professional cock sucker worked her lips, tongue, hands and neck like magic. Prince could only hold on to the sofa cushions and try to hold on. He could try all he liked but was no match for the hot head he was getting.

"I'm going to cum," he said rather politely for the circumstances. It was fair warning but only increased her pace. He increased his grip and nearly detached her tonsils when he exploded.

Sophia mumbled something intelligible with a mouthful of man and swallowed with loud gulps. She wanted to go to America, so she wasn't finished yet. Once she made sure he stayed hard, she rose and pushed him backward. He looked down and watched her wriggle him inside of her. She sank slowly until she was filled to capacity and began to ride.

The country girl grew up riding mules and horses before graduating to dick. Her intention was to put it on him so well, he'd take her home when he return. However, the thick dick inside of her soon got the better of her. Her body seized when a strong climax rocked her world. A gush of juice ran down her and him and pooled on the cushion beneath them. She howled in delight and slumped over, spent.

Prince knew enough from Sister Clara to take over from there. He rolled her over on her back and found a stroke of his own. The sixteen-year old only had one speed, fast and pounded her until she came again.

Sister Clara had two grown daughters away at college and didn't want anymore children. So she taught Prince the only birth control method available. He would stroke up until the last second and pull out. She would look down and watch him deposit his babies on her stomach instead of in it.

"Shit!" he shouted and snatched out. He loved the feel when she drank his seeds the last time, so he slid up and pushed back into her mouth.

"Mmm!" Sophia moaned as he spasmed and sputtered down her throat once more.

Claude had told her to fuck him to keep him busy but now she had her own plans. She would play along with his agenda while working towards her own, as well. She was still working it when Claude returned hours later.

"Hmph," Claude said as he walked in on the copulating couple. Prince tried to stop in embarrassment, but Sophia reached up and grabbed his hips. She kicked her own legs even higher and slammed him up and down, in and out of her. Claude figured they were going at it again instead of still at it from when he left. He watched for a moment before continuing to his room and closed the door.

"Give it to me!" she insisted when his stroke grew choppy and his breathing shallow. He was either dying or on the verge of another climax. She banked on the latter and constricted her pussy around his dick like a python. Pulling out of a tight, wet, hot vagina at point of climax is a superhuman feat in itself but damn near impossible when a woman squeezes.

"Argh!" Prince grunted and gave her what she wanted. He leaned directly on her cervix and exploded.

They lay there kissing and caressing while he went limp and slid out of her on his own. He finally rolled from between her legs, where he'd been all night. Sophia suddenly remembered the last part of Claude's plan and retrieved the money she was given.

"Here monsieur," she said with a royal bow and handed him the money.

"What is this for?" he asked, after accepting it. It was the first money he'd held in his hand since leaving America.

"For making me feel good. You should be paid anytime you please a woman," she explained as directed. She had been paid for her night off to spend with him, so she stood to leave. "Will you take me? To America?"

"Yes," he eagerly agreed. If this was life with her, he was all in. The sex was so good, it momentarily distracted him from the hardships of his life. They returned the second Sophia stepped from the house. Luckily, the hours of sex wore him out and sleep came to claim him.

CHAPTER 7

"Bonjour," Claude called as his stood over Prince the next morning after inspecting him as he lay mostly naked on the sofa. He was a wonderful specimen and would make him lots of money. He thought about having one of his sissies come over tonight to test him but decided it may scare him off.

"Bonjour," Prince greeted groggily. He looked down and saw he was exposed and scrambled to cover his impressive morning erection. "Excuse me."

"No worries. Get yourself together. Adelaide is preparing a meal," Claude said and turned to give him mock privacy. It was he who pulled the sheet away to expose the morning meat in the first place.

"Is my mother coming today?" he asked hopefully as he stood.

"Perhaps," Claude said to keep hope alive. Margaret would still be dead no matter when he told him, so he decided to wait until he had the boy where he needed him.

After a shower warmed by the morning sun, Prince joined his host for brunch. Claude danced around conversations, waiting to see if he would speak of last night on his own. He didn't, so he brought it up.

"So, how was Sophia?" he asked like a dare. In a sense it was since he knew she seduced him and knew she was wonderful in bed.

"We made love," he admitted. Then produced the money she gave him. "Then she paid me,"

"Yes, you must have made her feel good. A man should be paid anytime he makes a woman feel good. Or a man," he added like another dare. He noted the flinch and knew to abandon that market for now.

He had a few sissies on his team but needed a manly man for the married men who liked that sort of thing. Like it so much, they flocked to the small island nation in search of it.

"That's what she said kinda?" he said.

"I should get half since I introduced you, no?" Claude offered. It made sense to Prince since he wouldn't have gotten some pussy and some money if he hadn't been here. Half was still a whole lot better than none, so he gladly parted with it.

Claude smiled inwardly and outwardly as he accepted the money. It was his money to begin with but the investment had made dividends already. One more night and he would break even. Everything after that would be profits.

"Thank you," Prince said to all. The place to stay, the food, sex and money. Now all he needed was his mother.

******

Prince asked about his mother everyday for a week. He was given variations of the same answer but no closer to the truth. In the

68

meanwhile, Claude convinced him to explore his surroundings. He set out into the markets and sampled fruits and foods of the region. Being able to spend his own money gave the teen a sense of power. Just as Claude knew it would. He also knew how he would feel once his money was depleted.

Now that he felt the highs and lows of having money and not having it he was easy prey. Especially when having money was tied to sexual pleasures. The fruit was ripe, and hanging low. All that was left to do now was pluck it.

"Not going out today?" Claude asked when he found Prince staring at life outside of the window instead of immersed in it.

"I have no more money," he said with a slight whine. Money wasn't required to explore but did make it better.

"I see," Claude said and slipped into thought. His fingers snapped when a preloaded idea popped up. "I know where you can make some money."

"Sophia?" Prince asked and felt his dick jump below. He longed for her return almost as much as his mother's.

"No," he said sadly even though it was him who kept her away. "I know a woman from abroad, Canada. She would surely pay you for a good time?"

"Okay," Prince agreed since he wanted some pussy and money just like any sixteen-year old boy would.

"Fine. I'll arrange it for tonight," Claude said as if it hadn't already been arranged. "Of course we will split the proceeds since I am making the introduction, no?"

"Yes," Prince corrected. The promise of money made his day, so he set out and did some more exploring. Now if he saw something he liked, he could just return tomorrow and buy it.

He returned for dinner and got dressed for his first date. Claude loaned him some appropriate clothes and helped him get ready. He knew young Prince could handle himself in the sack since Sophia was begging to come back for more. Even offering to pay her own money for another night with Prince.

"You'll be spending the evening with Miss Banks," Claude explained. He probably should have explained more but Prince would figure the rest out when he got there.

"Is she pretty?" Prince wanted to know. He had been asking about Sophia just as much as she was asking about him.

"So just do whatever she likes, for as long as she likes," he said, ignoring him as led the way outside. The watchman glared at Prince as they got into the car and pulled away. A few minutes later, they arrived at the international hotel favored by international guests.

"Okay," Prince said as he watched the city out the window as they rode.

"Whatever she likes, she's paying for it," Claude reminded and gave him the room number.

"Okay," Prince agreed once more and followed him inside. Claude paid the doorman, so Prince could enter then left him on his own.

"Room 229," Prince told the door man who looked him up and down. He gave a "better you than me" shrugged and pointed him towards the stairs.

Prince moved quickly up the flight of stairs. The sooner he got there, the sooner he could get some much needed sex.

"Bonjour!" a woman's frilly voice sang in reply to his knock. He heard heavy footsteps rushing towards the door.

"Bonjour!" he called back with a smile but it vanished when the door was snatched open. He could only hope the large white woman with bleached blonde hair and wrinkled skin wasn't Miss Banks. "I'm here to see Miss Banks?"

"You're seeing her, honey!" she laughed heartily and struck a pose. The light from behind her shone through her thin gown and made matters worse. Prince stood there blinking as his mind scrambled to come up with his next move. The walk to Claude's house was far too far. Plus, he would be mad at him and might not let him back in. Where would he stay then, how would his mother find him when she came for him? He was still pondering when she pulled him inside and closed the door behind him.

"Claude was right. You are gorgeous," she gushed as she inspected him. She was definitely going to get her money's worth out of him.

"Um, thanks," he said and knew why Claude didn't answer when he asked if she was pretty. The fifty year old was actually pretty a few decades and hundred pounds ago.

Now her sun damaged skin looked more like leather and brown roots from her scalp betrayed her blonde hair. Her large rear end and belly stuck out from both sides.

Miss Banks paid for meat, not talk, so she took him into her bedroom and lifted the gown over her head. Prince blinked again at her lumps and wondered how he would ever get an erection to do what he was there to do.

She solved his dilemma when she helped him out of his clothes and into her mouth. Prince learned a lot about pleasing a woman that night. He also learned a lot about himself, as well. Lastly, he learned not to judge a book by its cover either because she had some good pussy. It would take fifty more years before he got some pussy better than Miss Banks.

The woman spent her entire vacation with him inside of her and paid handsomely for it. Prince almost hated when it was time for her to leave.

*****

72

"So, what do you plan to do with all that money?" Claude asked Prince. Not that he cared but he wanted to reiterate the fact that he had money and he was the reason for it.

"I will hire a driver to take me to the village. I have to check on my mother," Prince insisted. Claude heard the tone and knew he wouldn't be talked out of it. "She sent word. Said it's still not safe. They think you hurt that girl. They will kill you!" he said, trying anyway.

"I don't care. It's been weeks. I must see my mother," he insisted. Claude was a liar but was telling the truth about the village. According to Sophia, the mood was still the same. All talk was about the American who came and took one of theirs away. The men of the village all bragged about how badly they would kill Prince. Even the ones responsible for Antoinette's death.

"Let me go first," he insisted. Anyone who has ever had a goldmine knows you do whatever it takes to keep it. He would not lose his when he just struck gold.

"Bring her back or I will hire a driver to take me!" Prince repeated. Claude nodded and agreed as he backed out of the bungalow.

"Shit!" he fussed when he got outside. He couldn't stall any longer and had to come up with a plan. He plotted the whole drive out to the village but still hadn't found one yet, so he looked for Sophia.

All eyes were on the strange vehicle when it pulled into the dusty village road. The only car in the village now belonged to Franco along with the best house. He also laid claim to the right to lay pipe to Marquis's new widow. Claude wasn't a total stranger since he picked up and dropped off various girls over the years. He always said the sheltered village girls made the best whores for whatever reason. There were plenty since Margaret twenty years before up to Sophia today. The growing crowd of men flocked towards the house when he pulled to a stop.

"I am looking for Margaret. She has not been to work," he said as if he didn't already know what happened just as the elder stepped from the house he inherited like a hermit crab.

"Who are you?" Franco asked skeptically. They didn't get many outsiders inside the village but his car had been seen coming and going for years. The men and boys surrounded him in case they he didn't like the answer.

"I am Claude. Margaret worked in my store. With her," he said when Sophia came rushing forward. He realized then, he shouldn't have come here. He could have driven around and made up a story to tell Prince.

"Wait!" she called out as she ran up before they could kill him too. She may have saved his life but he was still going to lose some skin.

"Margaret brought death to our community. Do not come back," he said and gave the nod that started a beat down. The men and boys punched and kicked him into a fetal ball before Sophia managed to get him into his car. She had to drive since he left his senses on the dirt road.

"Why would you come here?" she asked as she sped away. She stifled a smile since he couldn't stop her from getting to Prince now.

"Better me than him. He wanted to come," Claude revealed. His bumps and bruises were proof that Prince couldn't return. The beating actually worked in her favor since she wouldn't be safe there anymore. Claude couldn't keep her away from him anymore.

"Are you okay, boss man?" the watchman asked when Claude staggered out of the car. Sophia had to help him out and up to the house.

"Do I look okay?" he snapped and went inside. The silly question was echoed by Prince when they walked inside.

"Are you okay?" he asked, then tuned him out when he registered Sophia with him.

"Yeah I...," he began then trailed off when he saw them making googly eyes at each other. "Fix us a drink."

"Okay!" Sophia snapped and snapped to it. She remembered how the strong drink kept him long and hard. The trio quickly downed their first drink, so she poured another. Claude waited until they reached their third before speaking.

"No other way to say it but to say it," he croaked. Sophia held her breath at what she knew was coming. Prince seemed to know too and began to frown.

"Your mother is dead. They blame you for the girl's death. They almost killed me!"

"They did," Sophia cosigned and nodded as Prince just stared off into space. The news didn't come as much of a shock since nothing but death could keep her away from her only child.

Sophia gave Claude a nod that sent him to his room. The door was barely closed behind him before she had Prince in her mouth. She worked feverishly to get him off and relieve the pain. She clamped her full lips on the head and jacked his dick like she was mad at it.

Between the grief and liquor, Prince was numb. The orgasms barely registered to him when he exploded in her mouth. It did do the trick and put him quickly to sleep.

Prince blinked the new day into focus. His morning erection throbbed and got his attention. Sophia stirred next to him and got his attention. A mix of lust and rage propelled him on top of the woman.

"Oh!" Sophia shrieked when he snatched her legs wide and plunged inside. The sharp pain was soon replaced by pleasure when her body had time to respond. Her juices began to flow and eased his in and out stroke. His misdirected anger propelled him up and down inside of her.

Claude had just stepped out of his room to relieve his bladder and saw the savage sex. A sly smile spread on his face as he watched the beast in motion. The kid was a goldmine and it was time to exploit him for all he was worth. He just hoped Sophia didn't get in his way. If she tried, she would end up with Margaret.

CHAPTER 8

Prince turned seventeen inside of Sophia's mouth. That's pretty much where he spent most of the last week since learning of his mother's death. Time passed in a blur of alcohol and sex, but it was now time to go to work.

"Save some for Mrs. Vladimir," Claude said from his chair.

"I was just warming him up," Sophia laughed when she released her lip lock on his dick.

"Well go wash the cum out your mouth and get to work yourself," he barked. Claude had been lenient since giving the bad news, but playtime was over.

"Okay, I'm ready," Prince agreed, mainly because he wanted some money. Claude made sure to keep them both broke and almost hungry. They could lay around fucking each other for free or get out and get some money. They both chose money.

"That woman is creepy," Sophia added when Prince went to dress.

"She pays well though," Claude said. That was worth the rumors of male escorts who were never seen again after.

The wealthy woman hailed from Eastern European country but kept an estate in Haiti. Rumors swirled about her being a witch or voodoo priestess but the truth was far more sinister. Even the male escorts who were seen again refused to go back. It was said they only survived because they pleased the woman. The ones who did not were not seen again.

"I'm ready," Prince announced when he stepped back into the room.

"Yes, you are!" Claude gushed when he saw his dressed in a suite and tie. This was a wealthy and sophisticated client so he had to look the part.

"Me too," Sophia groaned since she to go to the bar to sleep with sailors and tourist. Claude stood and led the way out to his automobile.

The first stop was the bar since it was closest to the bungalow. Claude wisely took the roundabout way out to the Mrs. Vladimir's home since the shortest route would pass the village. He guessed correctly that Prince would have jumped out and went to avenge his mother. He would have too and would have died trying.

"Wow," Prince said when they arrived at the medieval looking house. It looked even darker than the pitch black of the dark night.

"Yes, wow," Claude echoed. He didn't even take the car out of gear since he had no intentions of going in. "I will see you in the morning."

"Okay," he said and hopped out. Prince was still too young and naive to act on the danger he felt. The hairs on the back of his arm stood straight up as he neared the door. Still his desire for sex and money urged him on. The door opened as he raised his hand to lift the ornate gargoyle knockers. He almost felt cheated that he didn't get to try it.

"Mrs. Vladimir?" Prince asked, even though his own head shook "no" at the black woman who opened the door. Rich black women didn't do sex trips abroad back in these days, so his clientele was strictly white women of various heritages. England, Canada, France, Soviet, and now, Transylvania.

"This way," the Haitian maid instructed and turned around. Prince enjoyed the view of her shapely ass, wobbling beneath the white dress as he followed her through the dark house into a dimly lit den. She pointed to a sofa and demanded him to, "Sit. The lady will be with you soon."

"Okay," he said as a black cat slinked into the room. It stared up at Prince as if it were checking him out. It must have like what it saw and began to rub against his leg and purr. Prince gently scooped it up and stroked its fur. "Bonjour, pretty kitty. Aren't you sweet!"

The cat purred louder and seemed to relish in the attention. It rubbed its face against his crotch then nuzzled his cheek. It purred once more, then suddenly bolted as cats tend to do. It must have had a feline emergency and ran out of the room. A second later, a stunning white woman appeared in the doorway. She and Prince locked eyes for an awkward moment before she spoke.

"Did you enjoy playing with my pussy ?" she inquired and cocked her head for a reply.

"Huh?" he asked nervously then regained his cool composure. He hit her with his best smile and asked, "Isn't that why I'm here?"

Prince stood so she could check him out while he checked her out. Little did he know, she already checked him out. There was a set price for his time but going the extra mile always earned some extra money. Money he would not have to split with Claude. She stepped forward and extended her hand to formally make his acquaintance.

"Katrina Vladimir," she said and lifted a perfectly arched eyebrow in question.

"Prince," he said and kissed her hand. He was slightly taken aback by the coldness of her skin but maintained his cool, calm. She was beautiful with bright, white skin and dark, black hair. Her eyes were as black as the night sky and had a hypnotic pull. Prince felt totally stuck until she spoke and allowed him to move.

"Would you like a drink, my dark Prince?" she asked and moved to pour it. The question was rhetorical since she knew alcohol helped men last longer. She wanted him to love her long time and helped her own cause.

A smile spread on his face to the nice addition to his name. He nodded and accepted that he was now the Dark Prince. The candlelight shining through her dress directed his attention to her shapely ass and legs.

"Thank you," Prince said as he accepted the glass. He took a polite sip as they locked eyes once more.

"Come," she said, indicating that playtime was over. He tossed the liquor down his throat and accepted her cold hand once again.

They ended up in a bedroom with a large poster bed, with sheer satin flowing in the breeze. She pulled her gown over her head and revealed a perfect body. The most perfect body he'd seen life. His show was over and hers began when she sat on the edge of her bed and ordered him to undress.

Prince felt confused as his body automatically obeyed her command. He planned to take his clothes off for her the moment he put them on but now felt compelled against his will.

"Very nice," she nodded as his thick dick began to rise like the sun. She scooted back to the middle of her bed and spread her milky white thighs.

"Very nice," Prince repeated and smiled as her pretty pussy seemed to pucker up for him.

"Lick it," she demanded. Prince mentally declined like always. One hundred percent of his customers requested he go down on them but he always refused. No matter how much of a tip they offered.

Katrina didn't offer any tip or extra credits. Instead, she reached down and parted her outer lips to show him what he was after. Once again, Prince felt compelled against his will as the vagina pulled him in like a force field. His tongue replaced her fingers and explored her outer and inner labia.

This woman let out a loud hiss that should have scared him. She lifted her legs high in the air and bucked against his mouth.

Any misgivings he had about eating pussy slipped away as he ate. Eating pussy is not just a meal, it's an adventure. Better than one of those dinner theaters were people dress up like knights of old and damsels in distress. He was officially a pussy eater when she came with an eerie howl and filled his mouth with her sweet juices.

He didn't need permission to kiss his way up to her mouth and insert his dick in her life. The woman licked his face clean as he searched for a mutually beneficial stroke.

"There. Right there," she directed when he found it. She pulled his face down so she could put her tongue into his mouth. Prince frowned when he returned the favor and put his tongue in hers. He felt the super sharp fangs and pulled his tongue away.

"On your back," she ordered and he complied. Katrina mounted his dick backwards and sank until he reached the bottom of her well. She reached forward to grab his ankles before taking him on the ride of his life.

Prince had brought out the animal in most of the women he bedded. He even had

Sophia barking like a dog while he hit it doggy style, but this was different. This scared young Prince to his core.

Katrina's body seemed to move faster than humanly possible as she bounced up and down on his dick. She was as deep inside of him as he was in her. He felt a puddle form beneath him from the river flowing from her vagina. She chose to ride him backwards so he couldn't see the long fangs as they came out. Only because he would survive this encounter. In latter days, women took to social media if the dick was whack. Katrina would simply sink her fangs into his jugular veins and literally suck the life out of him. Instead, she rode him to orgasm after orgasm.

"I can feel your anger. Your hate!" Katrina shouted and squeezed him tightly with her walls. The hostility within Prince turned her on even more and got her off.

Prince was angry inside at all the hits he had taken already in his short life. First, losing his father then their house. Then being deported and losing his girl and grandmother. Now they took the only person he had left and he was angry. Not being strong enough to fight back, made him even angrier. He grabbed her waist and slammed her up and down while thrusting upwards with all he had. He had plenty too and Katrina bust another nut on it.

Prince got off himself but willed himself to stay hard as if his life depended on it. It did since she fed on those who couldn't please her. He couldn't recall how or when the episode ended but found himself alone in the huge bed when dawn crept through the window.

"Bonjour Monsieur?" the maid asked as she nudged him awake, only after taking a few minutes to examine the meat hanging between his legs.

"Yes? Where is?" Prince asked as he tried to get his bearings. He looked around the room as bits and pieces of the wild night came back to him. He head shook from side to side since none of it made sense. "Mrs. Vladimir?"

"She is gone. She said to give you this," the woman said and handed him a thick stack of Haitian money. More money than the maid had seen her give any of the men who survived.

"But where—" he began but got cut off aggressively by the maid.

"Where is none of your concern! Leave now, never return!" she warned. Prince opened his mouth to protest but she wouldn't allow it and screamed, "Leave!"

Prince didn't need to be told a third time and scrambled to get dressed. The maid got a parting picture of his meat before it disappeared in his clothing. He shoved the extra cash he earned into his pocket and walked out of the house.

Claude hadn't arrived yet, so he decided to set off on foot. Last night was creepy and he wanted to put some distance in between him and the haunted house. He had no idea which way they came, so he looked both ways and decided to go in the wrong direction. The direction of the village that wanted him dead or alive so they could kill him. Prince was only a mile away from his demise when a Claude pulled to a frantic stop in front of him.

"Get in the car!" he screamed as he jumped out of the car and snatched him in more like a kidnapping than a ride. He ran back around, hopped in and pulled a U-turn to get away.

"Um, what?" Prince asked once he finally slowed down to a normal speed.

"You were going the wrong way," he said calmly, but it didn't match his panic of a few minutes ago.

Prince took note of his surroundings and memorized the way back to Katrina's home. Despite the severe warning, he knew he would be back. He had to come back.

CHAPTER 9

"Whew!" Sophia grunted and came all over Prince's dick. He immediately pulled out and picked his book back up. The same book he studied religiously since his night with Katrina over a month ago. He'd been so engrossed in the book, she practically had to take the dick. "Really?"

"I knew it! I know it!" he said to himself as if he had been alone. His vampire books had long been his favorites but now had new meaning. There were too many similarities, too much explained the odd night. Now he just had to get back over there to confirm his theory.

"Finished?" Claude asked when he stepped back out from his room.

"I'm not, but looks like he is," she pouted. Prince hadn't even registered that he came out, let alone spoke.

Claude shook his head at him and his book, then again at Sophia's midsection. It was rounding out a bit and that could only mean one thing. The woman was a pro, so that only added up to one more thing. The only person capable of putting a baby in her belly was sprawled out on the floor with comics and books about vampires.

A baby would mean valuable down time for her and that wouldn't do at all. He knew Prince was oblivious to her condition, while she was trying to hide it. She figured if she made it far enough, Claude couldn't make her abort it. However, nothing was too far in this country.

The witchdoctors would pull a baby big enough to crawl from a woman if the price was right. He couldn't be sure which way the boy would lean, so he'd wait until he had her alone. That would be in a few hours since he had a huge white woman who would pay like she weigh to get laid.

"Oh, bonjour," Prince greeted when he finally looked up and saw Claude had entered the room.

"Bonjour," he replied dryly but he was already gone into the next book. "I hope you have some energy left for tonight."

"Mrs. Vladimir?" he asked so eagerly Sophia crossed her arms and pouted.

"No, for the hundredth time. Miss Rutledge is in town and requested no one but you," Claude explained.

"Please don't let her get on top, baby!" Sophia said and squealed with laughter. Once again, the joke was wasted on Prince knee deep in his studies. She was quickly getting used to it and turned to Claude. "Anyway, what you got for me?"

"A special appointment. I'll tell you all about it later," he said and set out to set up that appointment. Sophia dropped below Prince's waist and gave him something he couldn't ignore. He sat the book down and went for round three of the day.

*****

"Have fun," Claude called out as he dropped Prince off at the international hotel.

Prince turned back and twisted his lips at the joke. He was here to have sex, not fun with a four hundred pound woman. Sophia cracked up at his expression and off they went.

"So, who you got for me?" she asked as they pulled away. Claude paused for a second and decided.

"Me," he said and unbuttoned his pants. Sophia cocked her head curiously and wondered if he was serious. He very rarely got high on his own supply by fucking his women. It had been years since he'd been inside of her.

"Have you forgotten how to suck a dick?" he demanded and wiggled his worm.

"No, I just..." she explained but what was there to explain. She didn't own a pair of Nikes but still decided to just do it. She leaned over and took the soft dick into her mouth. She felt it grow thick and stiff on her tongue. Nowhere near as thick or stiff as Prince, though, but she began to work her neck.

Claude forgot how hot the young village woman's mouth was. She reminded him of Margaret when she was that age. He nodded with his mental decision to pull another poor girl from one of the poor villages and put her to work, as well.

"Magnificent," he marveled at how good her head was. No wonder she pulled in so much money. He had to slow down a little so he wouldn't reach their destination before he reached his.

Sophia felt him began to twitch and knew the end was near. She reached for a "handickerchief" since only Prince had the right to cum on her tonsils. Claude had other plans, grabbing the back of her neck and holding her in place.

"Magnificent!" he repeated with a grunt and filled her mouth with salty semen. Sophia grunted and squirmed as he pumped her mouth full. She refused to swallow and let his cum come back out of her mouth and on his pants.

"Ugh!" she said and spit when he released his grip. He wanted to be mad but man, could she suck a dick. Besides, if anyone had the right to be mad it was about to be her.

"Come on," he said and opened his door. He was already knocking on the door when he realized Sophia hadn't budged. Little did he know, she knew what this place was. "What are you doing?"

"I'm not going in there! She's not right. She will harm me!" she said in terror.

"Get out of my car then. You want to have a baby, then find somewhere to live!" he demanded. The woman of the house opened her door and watched the exchange. "Go back to your little village and eat iguanas and mangos!"

"But Prince?" she moaned. She would go back and would eat iguanas and mango as long as Prince went with her. She knew that wasn't an option though because they would both be stoned to death and beyond.

"Prince is a boy, a child. You really think he wants a child? He doesn't!" he shot back.

"He doesn't?" she asked curiously. She never thought about that part. Women had trapped men with babies since cavemen and cave women and cave babies.

"No, he doesn't," Claude said and softened his tone when he saw his way in. "We talked about it just recently. He will be returning to America one day and wants to bring you. A child would be too much."

"It would, wouldn't it?" she asked as his reasoning began to make sense. She planned to just spring it on him too once her belly rounded out past the point of no return.

"Way too much," Claude said and extended his hand. Sophia looked at it for a moment before accepting it. He helped her out of the car and toward the house that doubled as an abortion clinic.

"Bonjour," the woman said and stepped aside so they could enter. The coppery smell of blood and decay caused them both to wince.

"Bonjour," Claude and Sophia greeted and followed her into the bowels of the house. The smells intensified as death and fecal matter got mixed in.

"Mppmh!" Sophia grunted when the smells overcame her. She looked around for a bathroom or trash can to throw up in but didn't have time. She leaned down and tossed up her dinner.

"Come," the woman said and led her into a room with a table in the middle. "Take off your clothes and get on."

"I'll wait outside," Claude decided when he saw the dangerous tools of her dangerous trade. Crude scrapers, and spatulas still stained with dried, flaky blood. Sophia looked like she wanted to cry as she took her clothes off below her waist. There was no clean place to put them, so she held them against her chest and laid back.

"Foots up," the woman said and helped her put her feet into her makeshift stirrups. She touched Sophia's vagina and caused her to flinch. "Be still."

"Yes," Sophia agreed and tried to be still and quiet but wouldn't be able to do either.

Claude almost felt bad when he heard the animalistic scream from the back. He would have certainly felt bad if he had witnessed the mauling taking place in the next room. The woman shoved a device into Sophia's labia to spread her wide. Next, she inserted a crude scraper with sharp blades past her cervix and into her womb. Another scream worse than the first one caused Claude to step outside.

"Be still," she repeated as Sophia squirmed and twisted on the table. The sound of tissue crunching and torn echoed as she scrambled the life inside her womb. The brutal procedure came to and end and she withdrew her tools. "You will bleed. Your pickney will come out with the blood."

Sophia was in so much pain she could barely sit up. The woman handed her an almost clean towel to put between her legs and sopped up the blood. It quickly filled, so she gave her another. She was in too much pain to dress, so she staggered out holding the towels between her legs. She had to lean against the wall as she walked just to stay upright.

"Are you okay?" Claude asked when she came out, even though it was clear that she wasn't. She was pale and sweating so profusely, he almost thought about taking her to a real doctor. Almost but that would cost more money on top of what he invested with the bootleg abortion.

"No, I feel weak," she admitted. Claude decided to nurse her himself and helped her into the car. He rushed back to his house and helped her inside. Until now, Sophia and Prince camped out on the living room floor but he decided to put her in his own bed. The sheets would just be another investment.

"Here, drink this," he said and handed her a tall glass of alcohol to ease the pain. "I'll be back. When he comes tell him you're period is on."

"But," she called after him but her voice wasn't strong enough to reach him by the time he reached the door.

Miss Rutledge had paid for half a night and that ended an hour ago. He wouldn't mind if Prince spent overtime inside of her as long as she paid. He rushed over to the hotel and used the back stairs to reach her room.

"He won't do everything I asked!" The large woman pouted when she opened the door for Claude. "I offered to pay him extra, too!"

"Lady, they haven't printed enough money for me to put my mouth on that thing!" Prince laughed. He was convinced Katrina hypnotized him when she made him go down on her. He longed to do it again but with her just her.

"Well if she pays extra..." Claude suggested, suggesting that he do it.

"You eat it then," Prince laughed over his shoulder and hit the door. Miss Rutledge batted her eyes seductively in hopes he would do it. Anybody, she didn't care as long as it got done.

"Not a chance," Claude laughed and hit the door as well. He was still laughing when he reached Prince at his car.

"No desert?" Prince asked sarcastically as they got seated in the car.

"We can stop for some because I'm not touching that thing with my mouth either," Claude laughed and pulled away. They bantered playfully the whole way home.

"What time will Sophia be home?" Prince asked. After a few hours inside of the doughy white woman, he wanted a little brown sugar before he went to sleep. He was still a child at heart and sex was his favorite toy since PlayStations were still thirty years away.

"She didn't go out. Wasn't um, feeling well. Bad period," he stammered.

"Oh," Prince shrugged. It had come as a relief since he knew she had been late. He missed the week of blowjobs that accompanied her monthly cycle. He frowned in confusion when they walked in and didn't see Sophia on the pallet they shared on the floor.

"I let her use my bed. It's pretty bad," he explained. Still Prince frowned since that didn't quite add up, as well. Claude cared for Claude above all else, so him giving up his bed didn't make sense. Prince and Sophia often had sex in his bed when he left them alone in the house. It was more for adventure and spite than necessity since they got to it just fine on the floor.

"Well, go on and join her. I will see you guys in the morning," Claude said and yawned deeply to prove how sleepy he was. It didn't make sense but he just made love to a four hundred pound white woman so what really did make sense.

"Sophiah?" Prince asked when he walked into the darkened room. The scent of blood reminded him of Katrina and stopped him in his tracks. A faint moan got him moving again and he went to investigate. "Sophia? Are you okay?"

"No," she moaned. He confirmed she wasn't when he saw yet another towel drenched in blood.

"Your period?" Prince asked in disbelief since he had never seen her bleed this much before.

"No. I won't lie to you. I did what you asked. Got rid of the baby," she said in a whisper.

"Baby? What I said?" Prince asked and leaned in as she whispered the night's events in his ear. He didn't know how to feel or what to think. Especially getting all the information after the fact. The only thing he did know was that Claude was lying to both of them. He played one side against the other while filling his pockets. To make matters worse, there was nothing he could do about it because he had no place to go.

"And, your mother. She died the day you came here. They killed her..." Sophia managed to say before drifting away. She slept with shallow breaths far between each other.

Prince lay beside her and cradled her in his arms. The long day and longer night caught up with him and rocked him to sleep. He awoke the next morning with a corpse in his arms. Prince's warm heart turned colder than the dead woman in the bed. He knew he had to bide his time but vowed to make them feel it. Everyone who wronged him would one day feel his wrath. He had to get stronger though and knew just how to do it.

CHAPTER 10

"How is she?" Claude asked when Prince came out the next morning. He sounded genuinely concerned since this was his doing.

"She asked for you," he said and sat at the table since the food was served. Claude jumped up and rushed into the room while Prince picked her Sophia's plate and raked the food into his own.

"Bonjour," Claude called out with a grateful smile on his face. He wondered if she would make it through the night and spent the night second and third guessing his decision not to take her to the hospital. "Prince said you..."

Claude stopped talking when he reached her and saw her. He saw the faraway look in her eyes and knew she was faraway from here. Her cold skin suggested she left hours ago which made him wonder why Prince would say she sent for him. He wondered what she told him. The abortion? His mother? Shorting him on fees? He should have stopped wondering and ran for his life. Instead, he went back out and resumed the lies and games that got him put on a list. A growing list of those who owed their lives to right their wrongs.

"She, umm. I'm sorry but she is gone," Claude announced when he returned. The cook crossed her heart, so he did, as well. "I will handle everything!"

"Okay," Prince said with a shrug and kept on eating. His heart had grown as cold as the dead chick in the next room. The cook and Claude looked at each other, then back to him. Claude took it as a sign that she hadn't revealed his lies and relaxed.

They ate in silence then set off on their separate task. Claude had to set out and set up a decent burial for the girl he killed. Meanwhile, Prince dressed to impress and set off on a mission of his own.

Prince walked over to the busy market where everything was sold from fruits and vegetables to throats and vaginas. Voodoo dolls to shoes and even souls. Anything could be bought or rented, so he was easily able to secure a ride. Until he gave his destination, that is.

"Where?" the driver screeched louder than the screech of his tires when he slammed on his brakes. "I'm not going to that house!"

"Well, just get me as close as you can," Prince said because he would not be denied. The man looked him over and pulled off once again. He decided a mile away wouldn't hurt, so that's how far away he let his passenger out.

Prince second guessed his choice of clothing when he began walking in the brutal Haitian heat. It felt like one hundred and fifty degrees and one hundred fifty pounds of sweaty clothes as marched forward. His clothes were soaked and squishy by the time he reached the house. It looked as dark in the light of day as it did in the dark of night. More proof that he was on the right track. He caught his second wind and walked up to the door.

"Yes!" he cheered to himself when he got use the ornate knockers on the door. It was not to be, because as soon as he lifted one of the gargoyles the door swung open.

"What do you want!" the maid demanded furiously and stepped into his face.

"Mrs. Vladimir. I demand to see her!" he barked back. They went back and forth for a moment until he decided to bypass her and find Katrina himself. The woman pulled a huge butcher and raised it to send him with everyone he loved.

"Let him in," a voice called out and saved his young life just before she brought it down into his neck. The woman still wanted to stick him but did what she was told. She settled for shooting daggers as she stepped aside and let him in.

Prince ducked around the woman and headed back into the study where he met Katrina the first time. The same black cat eased in and began rubbing against his leg and purring.

"I know who you are. I know you can change shapes once you have the power. I know—" he began but got cut off when the lady of the house entered the room.

"Talking to my cats?" Katrina asked and lifted an arched eyebrow into a question mark. The cat had a cat emergency somewhere else in the house and bolted from the room.

"I still know who you are," he squinted, pointed and nodded knowingly.

"Katrina Vladimir. Estranged wife of Lord Vladimir of Transylvania," she announced with the perfection of having recited it for hundreds of years.

"Besides that. I know!" he insisted then cowered when she came near. It suddenly dawned on him that if he were correct she could very easily drain every drop of his blood and kill him. Luckily for him, she chose another route of distraction.

"What am I?" she asked and pressed her body against his. He was still young enough to be aroused by a strong breeze, so the full breast pressed against him got an instant reaction. She pressed her pelvis against his erection and flicked her tongue across his lips. "Who am I?"

Prince wanted to stay strong but it's hard to be strong with a hard dick. He joined the kiss and reached around to cuff her ass cheeks. She unbuttoned his trousers and hopped into his arms. The distraction did the trick and he lifted her off her feet and fucked her in midair.

Katrina leaned in so he wouldn't she her secrets. She pressed her lips against his neck but the flow of blood coursing beneath his skin brought them out. It was only the recent feeding that curbed her animalistic urge to feed. That, and he was laying some pretty mean pipe.

Prince held on as she threw her hips into overdrive and bucked like a wild filly. She let go and fell back, only supported by his hands on her ass and dick in her belly. The maid's eyes went wide when she took a peek inside of the room. She nodded in approval at how he was putting it down. No wonder she let him live.

A guttural howl cleared all the birds from the trees and announced Katrina's next orgasm. Prince held her for dear life as she thrashed about. He waited until the spasms subsided and sat her down without getting off himself.

"Now, I know who you are. You're a vampire. Aren't you?" he insisted once more.

"Yes!" she breathlessly admitted. The maid was shocked at hearing her actually admit it. That good dick and strong nut brought the truth out. Most of her guests found out the hard way, when she drained their blood from their body.

"I want you to turn me," Prince said with total conviction. He even lifted his head to expose his jugular veins.

"Turn you? What do you know about this life? You think this is a game? You think this is easy?" she hissed.

"I know you are strong! No one will harm you! No one can kill you! That's what I want!" he said with the rage that turned her on.

"It's a lonely life. Everyone you love will get old and die. While you stay the same age forever. I look thirty five years old but I am closer to four hundred!" Katrina moaned.

"Everyone I love has already died. I want to avenge them. I must avenge them. I will, avenge them!" he vowed.

"You still have no idea what you're getting in to," she softened and said. Hers was a similar story and she took brutal revenge to right her own wrongs.

"I know everything about being a vampire! I have all the books. Magazines and comics!" Prince said excitedly, sounding like the young boy he really was. He began naming the mixture of facts and fiction he gleamed from his material. "You get stronger by drinking the blood of mortals, and—"

"No. Blood keeps us alive, just as food does mortals. When we kill another vampire, we take their strength. There are vampire hunters from mortals as well as vampire," Katrina stated and he jumped back in. "The number one killer of vampires is other vampires."

"The more strength you gain, the more special powers you get. Shape changing, hypnosis, and... Hey! That's how you made me lick you down there!" he protested.

"Guilty," Katrina laughed, something she rarely did. "Yes, hypnosis. Fly like a bat, walk like a cat and more much more."

"Then, when you get strong enough, then you can become a daywalker," Prince said in awe. "Turn me. I'm ready!"

"Ready to be a teenage boy for eternity? Or until some grown man or woman vampire overpowers you and takes your life and power," she said and Prince nodded.

"Then I'll wait until I'm older. The day I turn 18!" he bargained. Ten more months shouldn't kill him and then he could go take what belonged to him.

"Let's say 21. In the meanwhile I have plenty to keep you busy," she said and led him to her bedroom. "Do I have to hypnotize you again?"

"Nope," Prince said and took position between her legs. He would gladly spend the next four years right here licking her labia in exchange for immortality and the strength to take his revenge.

Luckily, he didn't have to spend the next four years because it only took twenty minutes before Katrina came all over his tongue. His lips glistened like a glazed donut, so it was only right she lick them when he pushed inside of her. She took her juices right back as he built a steady rhythm between her legs. A mutual climax later and they both gasped for air.

"Time to leave," Katrina said and stood. It was a test to see if he had the discipline needed to be from the undead.

"When will you need me again? I'm at your service," Prince declared and stood, as well.

"I will send for you," she said and left the room. She left out the part about losing your soul. Even immortality has an end date and the hell fire awaits.

"Will you really turn him?" the maid asked jealously. The aches and pains of getting older were getting to her and she wanted to be immortal, as well. She'd been asking for years but always got rejected. The boy laid some pretty mean pipe and now he gets to get turned.

"Why yes, just like the rest," she said and laughed a wicked laugh. As they spoke, the gargoyles knockers began to knock. The maid bowed and scurried away to answer it.

"Bonjour, Katrina invited me for lunch," a handsome man explained when the door was opened.

"Of course," the maid smiled and stepped aside so he could enter. She scanned up and down the street to see who would be the last person to see him because he would never be seen again. He wasn't just here for lunch. He was lunch.

"Look who's here," Katrina cheered when her guest was escorted to her room. The maid took a final look at the handsome man since he would never look like this again. He was selected for sex and dinner just like men do except in reverse. Men whine and dine women so they can fk them. Katrina fucked them first, then dined on them. Unfortunately, Prince had fed her dick diet, so she skipped straight to the main course.

"Right on time," he smiled and began to undress. Katrina simply slipped her nightgown over her head and knelt before him. His dick throbbed to life right in front of her face.

Katrina smiled back, but unlike his, hers grew into sharp fangs. She gripped his ass cheeks firmly with her hands. He was helpless as she took half of him into her mouth and slammed her razor sharp teeth down like a guillotine.

"Off with his head!" she laughed but he couldn't hear it over his own screams. He tried to pull away but her claws came out and dug into him cheeks. She clamped on to what was left of his manhood and literally sucked the life out of him. When he fell from loss of blood, she went with him and drained him dry.

Katrina snatched the empty corpse by the ankle and dragged him down to the back door. Her pets went wild and howled despite the moon not being out yet. She was still susceptible to daylight, so she flung the two hundred pound man from the doorway. She had the strength of twenty men and a couple of vampires, as well. The ones she killed and took their strength just as she would do with Prince when the time was right. The wolves rushed in and tore off body parts for their dinner.

CHAPTER 11

"Bonjour! I'm glad you're back! I made all the arrangements. Paid for it myself!" Claude said when Prince arrived back at the house. Good thing he did or the grimy man would have gotten a refund and had her drug into the woods for free.

"Oh," Prince sighed. He couldn't mourn the woman but would miss the sex. His only concern now was getting older so he could be turned. The next three years and several months were a blur of alcohol and sex with white women. Including Katrina, who exclusively slept with him and fed off her other suitors.

Times passes whether you're having fun or not and Prince got older. Not as fast as he liked but older nonetheless.

Prince was smart enough to save most of the money he made slinging dick for Claude. Especially the tips he earned with the tip of his dick. He pleaded with Katrina to turn him when he turned 18 right after fucking her into submission. She declined, so he tried again at 19, and again at twenty.

Then he turned 21 and was a fine specimen of a man. The stereotypical tall, dark and handsome man with a deep baritone voice. He had been meticulously groomed by a woman who dealt with royalty for centuries. He was the total package and he was ready.

"I'm ready," he told a breathless Katrina after fucking her down real good. It always amazed and amused him that she could turn into a bat and fly around but still couldn't take any dick. He learned over the years that the best time to ask her for anything was after making her come real hard.

"You sure you..." she said, struggling to catch her breath. She too realized he waited to get her off real good before making a request. That's why she granted what ever he asked of her. Except this, this she wasn't sure of. She hadn't broken her word in a hundred years but wasn't so sure if she could do this.

"You gave your word," he reminded her after just giving his all. He couldn't read minds yet, but his powers of perception were impeccable.

"I did,'" she said and lifted her head regally. Her word meant a lot to her but so did Prince. To turn him would be to lose him. She would no longer be able to have her pet penis on call. He would either fly away or she would eventually eat him like she did all the rest. She had the power of a hundred men because she killed a hundred vampires over the ages. Half of which she turned herself.

Katrina nodded and they both stood from the bed. They faced each other and she flicked her long tongue on his lips. He knew not to join the kiss or he would end up back inside of the woman. She knew he knew that and smiled. Her super sharp fangs slowly grew right in front of his eyes. It was so sexy to him that his flaccid dick throbbed back to life between.

"You sure this is what you want?" she asked seductively as she lowered herself slowly in front of him.

"Yes," he said to being turned as well as the blowjob on the horizon. Katrina had a mean head game after four hundred years of practice.

"You sure?" she asked once more as she traced the thick, squiggly vein along the top of his dick.

"Aren't you supposed to bite my neck?" he wondered as she lined her fangs up with the vein. She slowly sank her teeth in just enough to draw blood. Prince winced but didn't protest. This is what he wanted. She sipped some blood then stood.

"Just a little taste. You would have made a wonderful meal," she teased as she stood.

Katrina tossed back the last bit of wine from her glass as used her sharp fingernail to open a slit in her wrist. She held the cup under and let a stream of her own blood fill it to the rim. She gave a mental command and the cut closed as quickly as it opened. She slinked forward and presented the glass.

"No turning back after this," she warned with a question mark. Prince answered her question by quickly lifting the glass and draining it dry. He didn't bother to wipe the blood from his mouth and smiled with the vampire version of a milk mustache.

"Now, what happens?" he asked since nothing seemed to be happening. He felt no different now than he did before getting bit on his dick and drinking her blood.

"Now, you die," she said casually over her shoulder as she left the room.

Prince felt something now as the pangs of death wracked his body and folded him in half. Death is heavy and the weight brought him to his knees. He writhed in pain as the painful events of his short life flashed before him. It was nothing but more pain as he saw his father, mother, grandmother, and Antoinette. They died once again right before his eyes. Then came the fire. A fire so hot he could feel the heat while still in the throes of death. A fire so hot he could hear the sun seeking refuge in Allah from its heat. Then silence.

*****

"Monsieur, he moved!" Claude's maid shouted when Prince began to stir awake. She rushed off to retrieve her boss as Prince sat up and tried to get his bearings.

He looked at his hands, then touched his face. He was alive but clearly remembered dying. He squinted as he took in his surroundings and wondered how he got here. His last memory was dying on Katrina's bedroom floor.

"Prince!" Claude shouted in relief when he saw he finally woke up. He had been asleep for a whole day right there on the floor. He didn't know how he even got back inside the house. He was just there he woke up. The maid rushed to open the blinds to light the sun shine in.

"Aaargh!" Prince screamed and rolled out of the direct sun. The maid frowned and crossed herself as usual.

"Close it! I see someone has a nasty hangover," Claude said. "Fix him a drink. We need you one hundred percent for tonight. Big spender!"

"I have plans for tonight," Prince said with a vengeful grin. This was the moment he was waiting for and that village was about to feel it.

Prince knew he had three days to either drink the blood of a mortal and stay immortal, or resist and revert back to normal. Katrina gave him a choice but he already made it. He was thirsty already and could hear Claude and the maid's hearts beating loudly like a drum. He would resist for now, so he rushed into the bathroom.

"Does he look different?" Claude wondered. He wasn't sure if he was taller, wider or what, but he definitely looked different. Larger than life.

"The devil is in him!" the old lady yelled in a whisper and crossed her heart once more.

"Shut up! He's fine!" Claude insisted because Prince was a goldmine. They both had piles of money earned from his strong back and long stroke. "Now shut up and cook!"

"Fangs!" Prince demanded in the mirror. He noticed how foggy his reflection was and wiped the glass. It didn't get any better and his fangs didn't pop out on command either. He tried various commands to get them to grow but nothing worked. "Grrrr."

Prince began to grow frustrated when they wouldn't pop out. What kind of vampire didn't have fangs? How would he exact his revenge or even stay alive if he couldn't drink blood? Then he relaxed and simply willed them to grow and they did. He made them go up and down as any kid would with a new toy. Next, his claws grew from his fingertips. He was as strong as ten men and could feel it coursing through his body. The Dark Prince was ready.

"Breakfast is served!" Claude cheered when Prince emerged from the bathroom.

"I'm not hungry," he said to both their surprise. Claude and his maid had watched the man sleep for a day straight, so he had to be hungry. The woman nodded at her suspicion that the devil was in him. She crossed her heart and left the room.

"So, will you be able to see Miss Banks tonight?" he asked gingerly since Prince just practically awoke from a coma. The truth was a little more sinister since he actually just returned from the dead.

"I have plans for the night," he declined and laid back down. He slept until the blazing sun made its lazy decent and summoned the night. It was payback time.

CHAPTER 12

Prince awoke once more and got dressed to kill. He made a mental note to get himself a cape like the vampires in his books, but settled for casual attire and comfortable shoes. Claude hated to see him leave since he might have to go service the large white woman himself. Either that or leave her for the other men who peddled meat to the tourist.

Prince stepped out and inhaled the thick night air. The sun was gone but a humid heat remained. He aimed his body towards the village and set off on foot. His strides were long and fast until he was one with the wind. A black blur in the black night. The thirty minute drive was covered in two minutes on foot.

"I'm back," Prince announced triumphantly when he reached the village. His first stop would be the house his grandmother once owned. The village elder was in the middle of helping himself to Marquis's wife. He watched curiously for a moment to see if the old man still had a stroke. He didn't, so he went on and interrupted. "I see you like things that do not belong to you."

"What? You!" Franco said when he saw Prince standing over him. He still managed a few more strokes before getting up.

"Me," Prince smiled to show off his fangs. He crossed the room in a blur and clamped down on his throat.

Franco couldn't even scream when Prince bit and pulled his Adams Apple, windpipe, and jugular veins away with one bite. The resulting gush of blood almost tempted the new vampire to drink. He wasn't here for that and let it waste on the floor below. Marquis's wife began to scream but he snatched her off her feet by her throat. He squeezed his hand until her head nearly came off of her neck. He flung the empty shell out the window. Franco was tossed out next.

"You're evicted," Prince told the corpse as he moved on to the next house. Sophia told him how the women joined the murder of his mother, so he didn't spare them either.

Prince moved through the houses with a deadly speed and annihilated everyone inside. He killed so quickly, their screams died in their throats allowing him move undetected through the village. He saved the men who killed his girl for last and entered Jon Paul's home while he slept. A sinister smile spread in his fanged mouth to match the sinister idea that popped in his mind.

"Wake up," Prince said nicely but delivered a brutal slap that was everything but nice. His open claws opened nasty gashes in the man's face.

"You!" Jon Paul announced and rose. He had blamed Antoinette's murder on him so many times over the years, he actually believed it now.

"Yes, me," Prince replied with another swipe that opened the other side of his face.

"What, are you?" Jon Paul pleaded when he realized he had a monster in his room.

"Why I'm the same thing you are," he replied and used a claw to open his own wrist. He forced it into the man's mouth and forced him to drink.

"What, what, d—did you do to me?" Jon Paul asked as the pangs of death suggested it was deadly. Prince replied by watching him die. He repeated this at the last four men's homes and turned them, too.

He still had enough time to rush back and bed Miss Banks. Not because he had to but because he liked to.

*****

"Two more days," Prince said when he awoke the next afternoon. If he abstained from drinking blood, he would return to being mortal. He was almost done with his mission and had a choice to make. Or was it being made for him, because he could hear the cook's heart beating in the next room. Then the smell of fresh blood wafted in the air like an afrodisiac.

"Shit!" Claude fussed loudly from the bathroom. He came out a second later, leaking from a cut he made while shaving. Prince groaned from the overwhelming desire to drain every drop from his body. He felt a thirst and hungry like never before.

"Ouch!" the cook shouted from the kitchen when she cut a finger along with the fish.

Prince knew he couldn't, wouldn't resist, and rushed for the door to run from the temptation but the brilliant sunlight stopped him dead in his tracks. His skin sizzled the moment the rays touched him, so he slammed the door and leaned against it. Claude and his cook also maid both cocked their heads curiously at his odd behavior.

"Him the devil mi tell you!" the old lady insisted. Another twenty-four hours had past and he still hadn't eaten.

"Are you okay?" Claude asked and drew near to investigate. A trickle of blood from the fresh wound sealed his fate. Sealed all of their fate.

"No, I'm not. She's right. I am the devil," Prince snarled and bared his fangs. Claude tried to run while the cook raised her knife. Neither got them very far when Prince struck. In a flash, he gathered them both and pinned them on the kitchen floor.

The woman tried to scream when Prince bit into Claude's neck and began to drink. However, the powerful pressure on her windpipe forced her to keep it to herself. He could feel the man's pulse weaken with every swallow of his blood. Claude was drops away from death when Prince let up and let him live. He was still thirsty, so he turned to the cook who crossed her heart.

"Does that work?" Prince asked sarcastically and crossed his, as well.

"I seek refuge in saint Ezekiel, saint Barnabas, saint..." she rattled. None would be of any help since they couldn't hear her. God's refuge is the only refuge, yet she called on everyone but him.

"I don't think they're coming," he mocked and added injury to the insult by biting her neck, as well. He drank her blood almost dry and stopped. Prince bit his own wrist and let the blood drain into their open mouths. Both revived for a while only to die anyway. When they awoke, they too would be just like him.

*****

Nightfall fell and Prince was back on the move. It was time to head back to the village and finish what he started the night before. He debated on using Claude's car since he was somewhere between dead and undead. Claude had long ago taught him drive but never let him borrow the car. He was pretty sure he wouldn't mind now since he had bigger shit on his plate.

"Nah, I think I'll walk," he decided and took off on foot. Literally since his feet barely touched the ground and he arrived in a flash.

"What's happening to us?" one of the survivors asked as they huddled in a decimated house.

"I don't know," Jon Paul asked himself. He vividly recalled being dead but now he was alive. Barely because he felt odd and an even odder thirst. The five men tossed around curious questions none could answer until a guest arrived to settle it for them.

"You're vampires now. All of you," Prince explained as he entered the room. The men recalled the last time they saw him and cowered in a corner.

"But, I don't wanna be a vampire," one whined. The others nodded in agreement since they didn't either.

"Well, if you resist the urge to feed for three days, you would revert back to mortal," he explained to their relief. Well, almost because his next words killed their joy. "Except, you don't have three days."

Prince once again was a blur of fangs and furry when he attacked. He also carried a wooden stake to help do the deed. The men only helped his cause when they huddled in the corner. One by one, they fell under the stake. He felt his powers increase with every life he took. Once again, he saved the best for last.

"I'm not going to let you kill me," Jon Paul decided. Being a vampire was better than being dead. He felt his new found power and stood tall. His own fangs grew along with claws on his hands.

"Good. I was hoping you would put up a fight!" Prince snarled and took a fighter's stance.

Jon Paul was a pretty good fighter and attacked. He was sure his lunging blow would strike since Prince didn't budge. It came up empty when he vanished into thin air.

"Missed me," he laughed from behind him. Prince laughed again at the look of confusion on the man's face. He slapped that look completely off with a powerful blow from his claws. He struck his own chin out and let Jon Paul strike the same blow on his face.

"Not that time!" Jon Paul laughed at his own handiwork when long, deep gashes opened in his face. Only Prince's wounds quickly closed on its own as if it never happened. He swung again and once again, Prince ended up behind him. This time ended like the first when Prince clawed his face down to the bone.

"I could do this all night!" Prince laughed. He could have, but didn't because Jon Paul's next miss would be fatal. He lured the man to strike and dipped under the blow. He popped up and struck his neck with his claws and took his head completely off. "But I won't."

*****

"Bonjour, madam, monsieur," Prince greeted when Claude and the maid literally stirred back to life the next morning.

"What happened to me? To us?" Claude asked when he saw his help suffered the same fate as he.

"The devil has turned us into devils, as well," the woman answered correctly, except there was no prize for a right answer. In fact, the opposite awaited.

"Yes, but not for long," he said almost apologetically then plunged the wooden stake into her heart. Prince felt a surge of energy from killing yet another vampire.

Claude had seen enough and bolted for the door. A warm smile spread on Prince's face as he rushed outside into the sunlight and caught on fire. The watchman could not believe what he was watching as the man burned beyond recognition in seconds.

"There's rules to this shit," Prince said but it was wasted on Claude who was reduced to smoldering ash. A Caribbean breeze whisked along and took him away while the watchman blinked in disbelief. He now had a very important decision to make. He could either believe his eyes and accept it or dispute what he witnessed.

In the end, he shook his head and cursed his lying eyes. Prince nodded at the right choice and closed the door. He needed a good watchman now anyway since he had just inherited a house and car. Vampires are nocturnal creatures, so he retired to Claude's bed to sleep the day away.

CHAPTER 13

A wolf howled in the distance signaling that night had fallen. Prince blinked awake and immediately felt a hunger and thirst. Not only did he have an unquenchable thirst for blood but an insatiable hunger for sex. Night was the new morning, so his night erection throbbed for attention.

A mental debate ensued as to whether he should hit Claude's bar for tourist and hope for luck or go to Katrina. The bar was hit or miss since he could end up with a four hundred pounder or a pretty petite. With Katrina he knew what he was getting. Her sex drive was extremely high and now he knew why.

"Huh?" Prince asked when his senses began to tingle. He was suddenly on high alert but didn't understand why. Not until a knock on the door explained things clearly for him.

"Excuse, boss. The woman want to see you," the watchman advised. He stepped aside so Katrina could step forward.

"I could feel you?" Prince asked for understanding.

"Of course you could. I could feel you, as well?" she answered and asked since she didn't understand why his presence was so strong. Stronger than it should be for the newly undead.

"Oh! I read that before! We can feel each other when in the same area. Like bats sonar," he said excitedly. He should be excited too since he was about to get some pussy .

"Yes, a warning because the number one killer of vampires is—" she began but Prince jumped in to finish.

"Other vampires," he said. He would know since he had six under his belt already. Claude deprived him of a kill by running out into the sunlight. The kills were still new so he didn't even know what powers he had.

"Shall we dine first or entertainment?" Katrina asked. She too was thirsty and hungry, as well. Seeing him shirtless with a large bulge in his shorts made her moist in an instant.

"Entertainment," he decided after looking her up and down. The cross breeze created by open windows pressed her dress against her firm, fine frame and pushed dinner to the back burner.

"Entertainment it is!" she agreed and pulled her dress over her head. He was stepping out of his shorts by the time she finished. He lifted her straight up above his head and lowered her onto his twirling tongue.

Katrina let out a deep moan as his tongue probe her vagina. Another one escaped a few minutes later when she exploded and sent her juices running down his chin. She did an acrobatic flip and ended up in an upside down sixty-nine. Her head bobbed furiously as she gagged herself on his dick. This wasn't head, it was throat. Esophagus even.

Prince felt his knees buckle when he felt her tonsils touch the tip of his dick. He held on and concentrated on devouring her vagina. His concentration waned momentarily when he paused to come on her larynx. Vampires give the best head and he remained hard as life in the Port a Prince slums.

"Now, for my favorite!" he said and carried Katrina into the bedroom. He chuckled at the thought of Claude complaining when he used to fuck Sophia on his bed. The wet spots she left behind were nothing compared to Katrina but Claude would not be complaining ever again.

Katrina knew that meant her riding him backwards, so she took position and lowered herself on the dick. She playfully took her time as she descended to the bottom of his dick. Once she reached her limit, she began slowly rocking. This was the bread sticks and soup before the main meal. As soon as it got good and gushy, she took off with superhuman speed and rode the dick like a horse in the Belmont stakes.

He recalled their first time when he thought his eyes deceived him. Now he knew why she could move so fast. Katrina came in succession but never let up or slowed down. She rode him for an hour before getting up.

"Your turn," she said and bent over for the back shots he seemed to love. Prince took position behind her and eased inside. That was all the ease she had coming before he took off and pummeled her pussy with perfection. He too could have gone for hours but the thirst propelled his pumps until he snatched out and skeeted on her back. She hadn't been pregnant in four hundred years but he just liked to cum on her back, belly, breast and tonsils.

"Now, we dine!" he cheered. He cheered again when she turned around and licked his dick and balls clean of his and her juices and come. "Shall we go on a hunt?"

"No need," Katrina said and walked naked to the front door. She saw the watchman watching them fuck from the window, so she invited him for a closer look. His eyes went wide when he saw her step out and beckon him in.

"Y—yes?" the man stammered as his eyes frantically searched her nakedness like he couldn't decide if her liked the freshly shaved, plump pubic mound or the huge breasts best. Even her hard stomach and pink toes vied for attention.

"We were wondering if we could feed on you?" she asked so seductively, his head was nodding before she finished her question. He agreed anyway and they held him to it.

The two vampires bared their fangs and let out a hiss that nearly stopped the man's heart. He swung with all his might and punched Katrina in her jaw. She replied with a viscous backhand that would make Serena Williams say, "Dayum".

"Point," Prince chuckled when he ended up at his feet. He bent down and picked the large man up with one hand. Katrina rushed to his side and they leaned in to his neck.

The watchman wasted a great scream when fangs sank into both jugulars at the same time. The unholy lovers locked eyes and sipped like young lovers sharing one soft drank with two straws. His legs kicked and arms flailed until he ran out of blood to fuel his muscle movement. They sucked so hard that his internal organs began to collapse. His cheeks and eyes sank in as a slurping sound sounded like the end of a drink from a straw. One person is generally food for one vampire but it did take the edge off.

"I could go for another," Prince shrugged as their dinner crumpled to the floor below.

"No time," Katrina replied and attacked. She took a viscous swing with her sharp claws that would have decapitated him with one blow. Decapitation works as well as a wooden stake. Prince ducked and frowned in confusion. A swift kick knocked him backward and ended his confusion. Katrina was trying to kill him.

"Oh really?" Prince laughed and prepared for battle. Little did she know he was stronger than she thought. A new vampire is easy prey to an older one, but his recent kills gave him strength. Not enough to beat her but he had a chance to survive.

"Really!" she laughed and attacked some more. He vanished and reappeared across the room. It was now Katrina's turn to frown since she couldn't understand how he got the extra powers.

There were no other vampires left on the island since she had killed them all. She turned and killed plenty over the years and was super strong as a result. Prince quickly realized he was no match for her and looked for his escape. She cut off his exit through the front door, so he made a dash for the window. He managed to dive through the window, shredding his face and skin on the sharp shards of glass. Katrina frowned once more when the gashes closed in and instant. She transformed into a bat and flew out after him.

Prince was smart enough to run to the busy tourist areas knowing she wouldn't expose herself in front of so many civilians. Her own survival depended upon her secrecy. She had been run off entire continents before arriving her on the small Caribbean island. She could just fly around and buzz his head until the roosters began to announce the coming dawn.

Katrina fluttered away and went home while Prince sought refuge in the hotel. He went up to Miss Banks room, but she had another hired dick for the evening.

Prince knew he wouldn't be safe here any longer. Katrina would catch him and kill him first chance she got. She had a four hundred year head start on him, so there was no catching her strength. He had to run.

He remembered the promise he made to his mother and knew it was time to return to America. He would go home to Atlanta and take back what was taken from him. First, he had to return to Claude's house and collect the ten thousand dollars he stacked over the years.

"She'll be waiting on me," he said in reply to the thought of returning to the house at nightfall. No, he had to go during the daylight if he wanted his money.

Prince collected dirty sheets from the laundry to try to cover his sensitive skin from the sun. Being a vampire gives new meaning to the phrase sensitive to light. After watching Claude burn to a crisp, he wanted no parts of it. He could smell the sex residue on the sheets when he covered himself. It beat the smell of burning flesh, so he shrugged it off and set out on his mission.

"Not sure if this was a good, idea," Prince said as he struggled under the sheets. The wind would lift a piece and cause him to burn. He would scramble to cover that part and expose another. Heads turned and watched the smoldering sight as he made his way to the house.

The scorched body print of Claude remained as a reminder in the front yard. Prince squinted curiously when he arrived to see the front door ajar. This was certainty odd since they went out the window last night. He went on high alert with fangs and claws as he entered.

"Yaaa!" Katrina's maid screamed and brought her trusty butcher knife down. Prince raised his hand and watched the knife go in to the tilt.

"She had to know you couldn't harm me," Prince said as he took the knife from her with one hand while lifting her off her feet with the other. The pressure on her throat prevented her answering so he eased off.

"She didn't send me!" she said and rubbed her neck. "She is furious! You don't know what you have done!"

"And I don't care. She tried to kill me. I want you to give her a message for me," he decided.

"What?" the woman asked and lifted her chin defiantly just enough for Prince to lean in and bite her neck. It sounded like he took a bite out of an apple when he bit her throat away from her neck. A blood stained smile spread on his face at the delicious blood spewing from the gaping wound. He spit her larynx out and clamped down on the spout and drained her dry. The hole in his hand closed and his burned skin healed as he drank.

Prince scrambled to collect his stash of cash as well his paperwork. He came across twenty thousand more of Claude's money and took that, as well. He dumped a potted plant out and mixed water with the dirt. He applied a thick coat of mud to the places that burned on the walk over. He covered himself again but this time he only walked as far as the car. There was only a few hours left before nightfall and he had no doubt Katrina would come for him. Especially when she found her maid empty and crushed like a discarded milk carton.

Prince drove over to the same port he and his mother arrived at years ago. He had the documents to travel on the passenger ship but it didn't leave until the morning. He would be dead by morning so he boarded a commercial vessel.

"Hey!" a man shouted when he spotted Prince sneaking aboard. "You can't stowaway here ya know!"

"I wasn't trying to stowaway," Prince said and raised his hands in surrender as he approached. He made sure to duck under the shade to avoid the brutal heat. Once the man was close enough, he used his vampire powers of hypnosis. "You will allow me to board for passage to America."

"I will do no such thing!" he insisted since Prince didn't possess those powers yet. He did have plenty of money, so he resorted to that.

"I'll pay," he offered and showed him the money. It had hypnotic powers of its own and commanded his head to nod. The thousand dollars he made was more than he would make in many journeys back and forth.

"Come," he said and led the way to a bottom level where several other men huddled together for the ride.

That smile wicked smile spread on Prince's face when he realized the ride came with a meal.

CHAPTER 14

Prince settled in the cargo hold along with the other stowaways. Men who paid top dollar to be smuggled to the land of milk and honey. Not all of them were going to make it since there was a hungry vampire in their midst. Others would be sorely disappointed since many wouldn't live any better than they lived in Haiti.

Prince relaxed once the ship pulled away from the port and settled in for the journey. He separated himself from the other men since the beating of their hearts distracted him. It sounded like a dinner bell being constantly rang. Most of the men paid him no attention and focused on the milk and honey on the horizon. Except one, that is, who seemed infatuated with the handsome loner. A big bully in search of someone to bully. Prince refused eye contact, so he couldn't ask him what he was looking at.

"Dinner!" the crew member announced as he came down with a pot of porridge. The men greedily filled their bowls so they could fill their bellies. Prince didn't eat but got in the back of the line so he wouldn't draw any attention.

"Too slow!" the bully teased and scraped the pot empty before Prince could get any. Ironically, he filled his bowl but just put himself on the plate.

"I'll find something," he shrugged and looked the chubby man over like one does lamb chops in the butchers window.

Prince felt a sense of doom when the sun began to set. He knew Katrina would be coming after him to finish what she started. Especially once she arrived at his home and find her maid. He ignored the rules of stowing away and came out on to the deck. He looked back towards the direction they just came from but couldn't see land. Instead he looked in the sky for angry bats.

"I have a long way to go," he mused when he compared his powers to hers. She could shift shapes and hypnotize as well as fly. He could still feel her powerful grip and realized it was only her surprise that allowed him to escape. If he hadn't turned and killed those men and the cook, he would have been dead too. He knew his survival deepened upon building his powers, as well.

"Then I'll be a daywalker!" Prince cheered at the idea.

"A what?" the porridge man asked as he came out behind him. Prince was so startled he practically jumped out of his skin and gave the man a good laugh.

"You can't be scared in America!"

"I know. I was born there," Prince admitted. Why not be candid since he wouldn't live long enough to repeat it. "Oh, and a daywalker is the most powerful vampire in the world."

"Vampires aren't real!" the man huffed indignantly. Prince just smiled and let his fangs hang. The look on the mans face would have been payback enough for taking his share of the food, but Prince was hungry.

"Vampires are very real!" he assured him in a final game of show and tell. His chubby cheeks spread to let out a scream for help but a scream requires a throat. His was quickly crushed under the tremendous power of vampire jaws. Prince took a bite out of his Adams apple and spit it away. He slurped down the refreshing burst of blood like a child squeezing a juice box.

"Taste like porridge," Prince laughed but the man didn't find it very funny. Dead people never do get the punch line, so he shrugged and tossed him overboard like an empty juice box. The bully made a satisfying splash when he hit the ocean. A variety of sharks learned to follow this route since men often found the way in the Atlantic instead of America. It was the land of milk and honey for the sharks.

Luckily for the rest of the stowaways and crew, it wasn't a very long journey from Haiti to America. Unluckily for Prince, they arrived in the middle of the day. He was forced to stowaway once again inside of a cargo container.

"Where are the other two?" the crewmember squinted and asked when his illegal cargo came up two short. He didn't bother searching too much since they all paid in advance. It wouldn't be the first time they came up short or even over at the end of a journey. In the end, he dismissed it and unloaded the vessel.

*****

Prince kept himself busy by trying to guess where he was headed as the box he his in was offloaded, then reloaded on a truck. The smell of bananas and tropical fruits reminded him of the busy markets of Port a Prince. An internal alert rang in his head when the sun dipped below the horizon.

The crate came to a bumpy rest once it reached its destination. Prince waited until all voices and footsteps ceased before emerging from the box. The humid night air of Miami was just as thick as Haiti but smelled better, fresher.

He nodded at his correct guess when he stepped out into a market. In a few hours, it would be bustling with predawn activity. That meant he had to secure a safe place for when the sun eventually rose. Luckily for humanity, the sun did rise because there were hundreds of vampires in America and they would feed until there was no one left.

Prince walked along the Miami streets in search of a sanctuary. He could go without a meal but had to find refuge. The smells of Haiti led him into the little Haiti area of the city. He had plenty of money so he checked into a seedy motel. He could afford better but better meant more scrutiny.

"Ten dollar," the clerk said and barely looked up at him as he rented his room. She doubled the price on him since she could literally smell that he was fresh off the boat. Likewise he could smell her monthly cycle had began so he rushed to get away from her before she became dinner.

"Ten?" he asked and cast a glance at the sign that said five dollars a night.

"Five for papers, ten without," she explained. Prince had papers but chose not to produce them. Instead, he paid the ten dollars from the large roll of money. The clerk's eyes went wide with the most dangerous combination lust and greed when she saw the money. The wheels began to churn as she plotted on how to separate him from his money. He would lose his life too if need be.

"Fresh sheets. Get some rest, you know," she offered along with the keys and a smile. Then she could use the spare key to sneak in and rob him.

"Yeah, rest," Prince chuckled and shook his head on the way out of the office. He hadn't yet developed the power to read minds yet but didn't need to since she was so obvious.

Prince winced from the sharp odor when he used the key to let himself inside of his room. His keen nose picked up the sex, smoke, and alcohol but on top of it all blood. He couldn't fathom how much blood had spilled in this room over the years but more was sure to come.

Not bringing clothes didn't stop him from jumping under the shower to wash the long journey off his skin. The water was far hotter than he experienced in Haiti and brought back memories of his home in Atlanta, the one stolen from his family and the one he vowed to take back.

"So soon?" he said when he heard a soft tapping on the door. He decided to answer as is, and stepped naked and wet to the door. He didn't bother taking a peep through the peephole since he assumed it was the greedy clerk.

"Bonjour, I—" a young woman began but got cut off by the dangling dick. It was what she was here for, but it still caught her off guard. The prostitute routinely worked the motel and spotted Prince when he arrived. She assumed he was just one of the Haitian dealers who frequented the place.

"Yes?" Prince asked and made his dick bob. It had her in a trance, so he commanded it to rise before her eyes. He summoned his powers of hypnosis and took a few steps back. "Come in."

"I..." she repeated in awe as his dick grew long and hard in front of her eyes.

"Put it in your mouth," he demanded and down she went. Literally and figuratively since she sank to her knees and took him deep into her mouth. Prince could have stayed in her hot mouth for hours but remembered it had been years since he'd been inside of a black woman.

Not since Sophia and Katrina and all of his paying customers were white women.

"Take your clothes off and get in the bed," he ordered in his hypnotic voice. She quickly complied, laid on her back and pulled her legs up by the back of her knees. He took a moment to marvel at the luscious black vagina and plunged inside.

The woman made a living selling pussy but he earned a discount with each stroke. By the time he finished giving her multiple orgasms, she felt like she owed him. That is until she stopped shivering and shaking from one last nut.

"Ten dollars," she said and stuck her palm out. Prince had plenty of money but decided to use his hypnosis for a freebie.

"I don't have to pay," he said, staring into her soul.

"The hell you don't! I don't run a charity!" she fussed and fussed until he found his pants and retrieved some money. Come to out he didn't have hypnotic powers yet after all. She just liked dick.

"Hmph?" Prince said and scratched his head. His shower was ruined by the sex, so he went back to finish what he started. Once he was clean and dry, it was time to feed.

Prince was debating on going out to find prey but prey came knocking on the door. A soft tap designed not to wake if asleep. The fanged smile came out as he slipped back into bed. He sat the roll of cash on the nightstand like baiting a mousetrap. The door eased open and in crept a mouse.

Prince was a nocturnal creature now and had excellent night vision. He peered through the darkness as the clerk searched for his valuables. The knife in her hand glinted dangerously in the dark. Her beady eyes lit up when she saw the roll of money.

Wait for it. Wait, Prince thought in amusement as she came to take the bait. She tiptoed closer and reached for the money.

"Gothca!" he said and grabbed her by her wrist. The knife wasn't for show and she quickly raised it and brought it down into his neck. Prince's eyes went wide and he died instantly.

Bodies were so often found in and around the motel, she didn't think twice about it. She snatched the cash and bolted for the door. Would have made a clean getaway too if a vampire hadn't been standing in the doorway.

"I killed you!" she shouted like she was mad he was alive.

"No, this is how you kill someone," he corrected and plunged his claws into her chest until he felt her beating heart. Prince collapsed on the woman and stuck his mouth into the gaping hole in her chest. He growled and snarled like a hungry beast as he drank her dry.

Once he had his meal, he checked outside to see if the coast was clear. It wasn't so he carried her to the back window and tossed her outside. He climbed out after her and drugged her empty shell into the woods. He remembered Katrina telling him to be careful of disposing with the corpses. She kept hungry wolves for just such a purpose. He didn't have any wolves so the woods would have to do, for now.

Prince decided to explore a little since several hours of the night remained. The dark Prince was a dark blur as he sped through the city. People could feel a whoosh of air as he sped through their midst. Something stopped him dead in his tracks when he reached the tourist area. An overwhelming force could be felt emanating from a nightclub. Prince knew then that there was a vampire inside.

The vampire inside was holding court with a bevy of beauties in the VIP section. He stopped and stood when he too felt the presence. A feeling he hadn't felt in years. There was only one other vampire he knew of in his city, but they coexisted. Still, this was his city, so he rushed outside to confront the intruder. There would have been a showdown on the sidewalk but Prince was gone. There would still be a showdown. It just wouldn't be tonight.

CHAPTER 15

Prince was grateful for the motels blacked out curtains once the sun began to rise. He was tucked away safely in the pitch black room, while the world basked under the bright sun. He slept peacefully until a noonday knock disturbed his rest. The intention was to ignore the knock but the knock wouldn't stop.

"Shit!" he fussed when he realized the knocker wasn't going to stop knocking. He unlocked the door then stepped a safe distance away and called out, "Come in!"

"Hello?" the prostitute from the night before asked and stepped inside. She scanned the darkness and spotted him before continuing. "Did you hear about Marvis? She was found dead!"

"Close the door," he ordered then asked, "Who is Marvis?"

"The clerk," she said, looking down at his crotch since that's why she was here. "I'm Olivia. I just wanted to see if you needed my service again today?"

"Seems to me, you want my services," he shot back. He was a sex worker himself and knew the value of the meat hanging between his legs. If he charged by the pound, he would be rich.

"I, I, umm," she stammered when he put her on the spot. Luckily, he let her off the hook and had another mission for her. He had visited the moneychangers last night and swapped out his Haitian money for some good ole American greenbacks. He gladly allowed the man to short him, but followed him home and took note of his address.

"I have a mission for you. I need clothes, everything. My bag was lost," he explained. He ended up repeating himself since the money in his hand distracted her almost as much as his dick did.

"What size?" she asked and locked in his sizes as he relayed them. He wasn't quite a mind reader yet but saw the thought that crossed her mind. She thought about taking the money and running off, but where? All roads ended up right back here in little Haiti.

"There is more here than in your hand. Come back and you can get more. Oh, and this," he said and sealed the deal by clutching the dick.

"Okay!" she nodded and rushed outside into the sun. Prince wasn't a betting man but odds were she would be back. He was right too because a couple hours later she returned loaded down with bags.

This wasn't her first time shopping for some man fresh off the boat so she knew he needed underclothes as well as clothes to go over them. Her taste however was a different story.

"Is this what the people wear here?" he asked when he pulled out the same colorful clothing guys wore down in Haiti. Claude had him dressing a little more international since he had international clientele. He actually enjoyed dressing dapper and debonair for his upscale clientele.

"Haitian guys? Yeah!" she said and held his clothes up to him to make sure they fit. She also produced take out plates of Haitian food.

"Thanks," Prince said in a melancholy manner since he no longer ate food for food. He sorely missed American food but would never get to eat it again. He sat his aside while she quickly scarfed hers down. "Have you ever been to the Capri?"

"The nightclub!" she reeled as if were on the moon. It was in the same city but still far beyond her means.

"Yes," he nodded even though he already had his answer from her reaction.

"No, that's for the rich and famous!" she said. Two things she would never be, turning ten dollar tricks in a rundown motel.

"Hmm?" he asked even though he had an answer. He was going to that club to have a date with a vampire. In the meanwhile, he picked the talkative girls brains about the city so he could learn his surroundings. He found it all very interesting, especially the part about the blood bank. A twenty- four hour blood bank that paid by the quart in an age before HIV people would come off the street and give blood with no questions asked.

The insatiable vampire and prostitute had several sexual bouts in between the conversation. Once the sun began to dip, he dipped into the bathroom and under the shower.

"Where are you going?" Olivia pouted when Prince returned from washing the sex away to get dressed. He put it on her so good, it confused her into thinking she had the right to ask him about his whereabouts. He cracked a faint smile that reminded her that she didn't. "Oh, yeah. My bad. I guess I'll go um, yeah—"

"Stay," he said like he had hypnosis powers. He didn't but she stayed anyway because she wanted to stay anyway. He finished dressing and headed out into the night. He planned to stay far away from the touristy part of town and the club where he sensed the vampire.

Vampires could be friends or foe but usually foes. Especially the alpha males when another one comes along. Katrina's words echoed in his head, "Vampires are the biggest killers of vampires". He needed to be stronger if he hoped to survive.

First off, that meant a steady source of food. Miami isn't like Haiti and he couldn't toss empty people around like beer cans. Katrina had been run off every continent on the planet for the same thing. She finally wised up after a few hundred years and secured a pack of wolves to dispose of the leftovers.

Across town in an upscale house, another vampire was preparing for the night, as well.

*****

144

"I wonder if I will get to meet him or her tonight?" Angelo said as his makeup was applied. The flamboyant vampire not only lived for the night but the nightlife, as well. He could be found in any of the cosmopolitan city's many nightclubs.

"Pout," his helper said so he could gloss the man's lips. Angelo pouted so he could get pretty for his prey whoever she or he may be. He would select, then wine and dine men or women his dinner. He loved to supply them with white wine since he loved the taste when he sipped from their veins. "Are you sure you saw someone?"

"Felt, not saw," he explained. Something he hadn't had to explain in decades. He licked his lips in search of a taste of the last vampire who happened upon his city. A handsome, European fellow who tasted like Shepherd's pie when he drank him dry.

"Perhaps it was Charles?" Angelo's handler suggested. Life was good as is and he didn't want anything to change.

"Charles! In South Beach?" he laughed at the ludicrous idea. "Oh, Ralph. Have you starting drinking already?"

"My apologies," Ralph said, pressing his lips tightly together to prevent anything else from slipping out and getting him in trouble. Angelo may have been an effeminate, bisexual but he had seen him in action. Seen a side of him no one else alive had seen. Mainly because they didn't live through it.

145

Charles was an elderly man when he was turned by a sarcastic vampire a century ago. While he hated being a vampire, he knew only hell awaited after his death. He killed to live and knew it would cost him his soul. In an act of penance, he opened the blood bank.

It saved lives in many ways since he provided much needed blood products for local hospitals, but it also kept him from feeding off the locals. Keeping the shop open 24/7 allowed him to work nights and hand select which donors to drink from. He was immune to the drugs and alcohol content in the blood but not the taste. The young and healthy had the sweetest and most nutritious blood.

"Well, I'm looking forward to meeting whoever this newcomer is. Hopefully, he will come back. Or I'll have to go find him," Angelo said and licked his glossy lips once more.

*****

"Have you given blood in the last week?" a nurse asked when a potential donor walked in to the blood bank. She knew some junkies or alcoholics would give 'til they had nothing left unless she stopped them.

"No," he lied since it hadn't been quite a week since Katrina drained some of his blood from a prick on his dick.

"Great. Fill out these forms and—" she was saying until Charles rushed from the rear and looked around urgently. Prince breathed a sigh of relief when he saw the elderly vampire.

Charles zoomed in on him as well and braced himself.

"I'll take him," Charles told his nurse when he felt secure that Prince wasn't here to harm him. He stepped aside and held the door so Prince could enter. Neither spoke until they reached his office. "You obviously know who I am, so who are you?"

"I am Prince. I'm just passing through. I don't want problems," he explained and lifted his hands in surrender as proof.

"You'll have problems if Angelo finds you. Have you eaten?" he warned and asked.

"No. Who is Angelo?" Prince answered and asked in reverse. Even though he was pretty sure Angelo must have been the presence he felt the night before. The feeling wasn't even that strong sitting this close to the vampire.

"What is Angelo, is a better question," he said, while checking the fresh pints of blood in the fridge. He smiled and nodded when he found what he was looking for. "Here we are. Nice blue eyes, blonde hair, all American Caucasian girl. College student, Red cross, peace corps..."

Prince inspected the plastic package and had to admit it was pretty. He was hungry and his fangs extended so he could feed. Charles watched with the enthusiasm of a chef serving a renowned food critic. Prince noticed the difference between puncturing flesh and veins against the plastic. It didn't have the same feel and flow of a heart pumping but he had to admit it was sweet.

"Ah ha," Charles cheered for his good selection as Prince sucked the pack completely flat.

"That is good," Prince admitted once he was done. He got back to the matter at hand and adjusted his question. "So what is Angelo?"

"A monster. A sadist who likes men as much as he likes women. Many vampires have come to Miami, but few leave Miami," he explained.

"He doesn't bother you?" Prince asked.

"I'm not a threat to him. He tolerates me because I keep to myself. I feed myself. Besides, he knows that even a vampire can gets redemption when killed by another vampire," Charles sighed.

"And he won't give it to you?" he asked since Charles's lonely sigh said it was so. He only remained alive for fear of the fire and Angelo wouldn't set him free.

"He's doomed and wants me to be doomed with him. That's the only reason he tolerates me."

"Hmph," Prince huffed and went silent as the wheels turned in his head.

"It's the only way you can defeat him," the seasoned vet said as he intercepted the thoughts bouncing around in Prince's head. "Kill me and take my powers!"

"Not today. I do want to meet this Angelo first," he said. Charles read those thoughts, too, and smiled at his plans.

"Another round!" Charles cheered and went back into the fridge for more blood. He came out with two packs and let Prince take his pick. "Nice black girl from the housing projects, or a rich housewife from Boca?"

"Black project chick, please and thank you," Prince said. They clicked plastic packs of blood and sank their fangs in for a meal.

*****

"Don't you want to go out? We can get conch fritters and—"

"No," Prince said and shut down Olivia's latest attempt to get him outside during the day. He had no idea what a conch fritter even was, but Charles kept him with a fresh supply of blood.

Prince finally did a little shopping in a Cuban shop that stayed open late into the night. He selected a suite and shoes suitable for the Miami nightlife. He had stalled long enough but knew he couldn't stall anymore. He'd felt the presence of another vampire over the last few nights and knew the time was up.

"Aw, man," Olivia pouted and poked out her lips. Luckily, Prince knew just what she needed to take the pout off her face. He pulled the sheet away and introduced his dick back in her life. The next few hours were a sweaty blur as they fucked until dusk.

"Here's some money for your conch or whatever," Prince said. He went into his stash in front of her face for the first time. It was the loyalty equivalent of a pop quiz.

"Okay! I'll get some for you too and..." she gushed until a knock on the door interrupted her.

"You must leave," he said and stood. His serious tone answered the questions she wanted to ask. She opened the door to leave and gasped at the larger than life figure in the doorway.

"May I enter?" Angelo asked rather politely. Olivia slipped beside him and took off on her mission.

"Of course," Prince said just as cordially. He was as prepared for battle as he could be since he couldn't possibly defeat him. The open back window was his only hope for survival. "I felt you a few times this week?"

"As I felt you outside of my hangout. Why are you here?" Angelo asked. Prince could literally feel him inside of his head and didn't try to deceive him.

"I am just passing through on my way back to Atlanta," he said and kept repeating it in his head so it would be the only thought he could read.

"With Daryl, he would enjoy your company," Angelo said and looked him up and down. Prince recognized it was the same look Katrina used to give. "How long have you been with us?"

150

"Not even a month," he answered and Angelo got the rest. Angelo frowned since his presence seemed stronger a freshly turned vampire. Had it been a lie, he would have known it, so he shrugged and continued his seduction.

"Ah, Katrina! I've known her for a hundred years. You are definitely her type. Mine, as well," he put out and waited. A smile spread on his face when Prince thought he would like that too. He read it would be a first, so he would go slow. "Since you're all dressed, come. Let me show you my city!"

"I was waiting for you. Let's go," Prince said and fell instep behind him.

Katrina may have turned Prince into a vampire, but it was Angelo who turned him on to the finer things in life. It was the wine and dine he used to seduce men and women. Neither had any need for the fancy cuisine of the city. Likewise, the champagne and cocaine didn't affect them but attracted attractive people to flock to their side.

The limos and flashy things is what got to prince. Being greeted and treated like royalty, everywhere they went was completely and totally addictive. Angelo saw the stars in his eyes and knew he was halfway there.

"Pick one. Any one," Angelo said as Prince scanned the Capri Club from his perch in the VIP.

"One, huh?" Prince repeated but couldn't narrow it down to just one. A gorgeous, jet black girl winked as she danced with a lovely Latina. A creamy white woman cracked an even whiter smile from the bar making his choice even harder.

"Pick four then. I'll help you out," Angelo said nonchalantly. Prince pointed out the three he had his eyes on and tossed in an East Indian woman who happened by. A snap of Angelo's fingers sent Ralph in motion. He was back in a flash with five since one girl had a girlfriend.

Prince was in awe once more when the limo pulled up to a gated mansion on the water. He decided he would live like this. If you must live forever, you may as well live well. The entourage entered the mansion and headed up the spiral stairs. They entered a room with a custom made bed designed to hold twenty.

"No clothing beyond this point," Angelo announced with a hand clap and began to strip. Everyone was here for the same purpose and quickly stripped. Ralph returned with champagne, cocaine and weed as party favors.

Angelo sat back and watched as young Prince dicked all five women into submission. One snored loudly while two more were balled in a fetal position once he was done with him. He knew he had him hooked to the lifestyle. Maybe he would let him live so he could make love to him next.

CHAPTER 16

"Olivia? Oh, Olivia?" Prince sang playfully as he entered the empty room just before dawn. Not that he expected to see her or his money when he returned, so he wasn't surprised not to see either her or his money. He shrugged his shoulders and got in bed to sleep the day away.

Prince's fangs and his dick grew as he dreamt about the night he spent with Angelo and company. The sexual orgy satisfied his hunger, then he and his host dined on the five women and quenched their thirst. The feeding frenzy had turned the room ruby red with tasty blood.

The dream switched back to the sexual part when he vividly recalled a fascinating blowjob. The dream was so real, he could feel the heat and pressure of a hot mouth tightly engulfing his meat. A little too real and his eyes opened to see Olivia trying to make up for stealing his money.

Truth be told, she really could not help herself. She was a snake and no matter how good you treat or how well you train a snake, it'll always be a snake. The girl couldn't even help herself not to help herself to the money, despite how good Prince and his dick treated her.

He let out a sigh and let her do what she was doing since she did it so well. A mortal man wouldn't have had anything left after the night he had. Of course, Prince was no mortal man. He would forever be a twenty-one year old vampire if he lived to be a thousand. He very well could unless another vampire came along and killed him.

Prince let her go for an hour before he decided to reward her with a mouthful of thanks. She swallowed, hopefully, that it would make up for stealing his money. It went to a good cause since she sent it to her family down in Haiti.

"I'm sorry," she said quite contritely once her work was done. The lengthy blowjob actually left her winded and out of breath. She cuddled up next to him like she would normally do.

"Yeah, I know," he said in acceptance of her apology. He still leaned her head back and clamped down on her jugular veins. Olivia squirmed in futility because she was no match for the grown man who happened to be a vampire.

He sucked down the delicious liquid lunch and felt her heart rate decrease. He almost went too far but managed to cut it off before ending her life. She was as close to death as one could be when he used a claw to open his vein. He let his own blood drain into her mouth until she was revived. She came back to life only to die so she could come back once more as the undead. In the meantime, he had some unfinished business with a moneychanger.

*****

The moneychangers are the human equivalent of the green gunk that grows in ponds and sewage treatment facilities. They take advantage of their own people because they're poor. Knowing illegal aliens couldn't go to banks, they taxed them fifty percent of any transaction.

As a result, Prince's money was cut in half when he swapped it for American money. He didn't protest when he saw the large rolls of cash the man carried. Then he drove away in a brand new 1967 Cadillac automobile. Prince was able to move just as fast on foot as he followed the man to his nice house on the nice side of town. He took note of the address for a later date and went back to the motel.

Tonight was that later date and Prince was back. He had to move quickly since he had a date with Angelo and what ever hangers on that would hang on for the night.

"Who?" the man asked curiously to the knock on his door. This was a time before cell phones and beepers, but he still seldom had uninvited guest.

"Me," Prince called back and the door began to open. Not fast enough for Prince so he kicked it, sending the man sprawling on his own floor. He knew this day would one day come and prepared himself for it. A shotgun was perched in the doorway for just such an occasion. Only problem was there was a vampire standing between it and him.

"You looking for this?" Prince asked and held up the gun. The man nodded his head up and down so he handed it over to him.

"Um..." he asked, trying to figure out what just happened. The robbery registered once more and he caught his bearings. "You come for mi, mi money!" he stammered.

"Yes. As a matter of fact, that's exactly why I'm here," Prince admitted. It must have been the wrong answer because the man lifted the shotgun and shot.

The blast lifted Prince off of his feet and slammed him against the wall with a thud.

"Well you can't a've it!" the moneychanger mocked and came near. He regretted that decision when Prince's grimace turned into a smile and his fangs slowly descended. The Haitian knew exactly what was happening and crossed himself as he backed away. "Katrina!"

"You know her?" Prince asked as he rose to his feet. His clothes were shredded, but the gaping hole in his torso closed right before the man's eyes. He realized the gun was useless, so he dropped it and made a dash for the back door. Good plan except that damn vampire beat him to it. He did a 360 and ran for the front door, but there was Prince once more.

"Come on!" the man shouted and put up his dukes. He knew he was going out but not without a fight.

"Okay then," Prince nodded respectfully. It wasn't much of a fight though and ended with

Prince locked on his neck, literally sucking the life out of him. Once he drained him dry, he set off in search of the stash. He found it and made off with the moneychanger's life savings. Not that he needed it since he didn't have a life.

*****

Olivia was somewhere between this life and that life when Prince returned to the room. She wasn't quite ripe yet, so he ignored her and changed clothes for another night on the town. He was so impressed with his new Cadillac, he would keep driving them for decades later. He was supposed to meet up with Angelo but had a quick pit stop to make first.

"Welcome," Charles greeted when Prince arrived at the blood bank. The new youth had breathed new life into the old man.

"Thank you," Prince said with a head nod as Charles produced a couple packages of fresh blood. "Is this it?"

"No. It's the appetizer," he said. "Remember to clear your mind. Focus your thoughts. I did not need to know about your visit to the money changer tonight."

"I understand," Prince said since he understood that his true thoughts could be read and would get him dead. He instantly went blank and put a smile on Charles face.

"You could have been a blonde!" Charles cracked up but the joke went over his

157

guest head. "Anyway, be careful. Angelo is dangerous. Very, very dangerous!"

Prince nodded again and stepped back out to his new car. He rode over to Angelo's house and got out. The door opened as he drew near and Ralph welcomed him inside.

"He is in the study," Ralph said and led him down the hall.

"Prince! So good to see you!" Angelo cheered and hugged him tighter and longer than a man should hug another man. He was delighted by the delight he pulled from Prince's mind. He was getting closer to where he wanted to be.

"I stopped by to see our friend, Charles. He sent his regards along with..." Prince said and produced the packets of blood.

"Ah, yes! He doesn't like to feed, you know? Sacrilegious but he does get the best plasma in town," Angelo said. A snap of his effeminate fingers sent Ralph scrambling for goblets to drink from.

"Doesn't like to feed?" Prince asked as if he didn't already know. Charles liked to feed just fine. It was the murder he despised.

"Our fates are sealed. We are children of the devil and hell will be our eternal home. It is, what it is, so enjoy it while you can. He wanted me to dispatch him so he could seek salvation. He'll get no such favor from me!" he explained as Ralph poured the red blood like red wine. The high society vampire lifted the vessel to his nose and inhaled sharply. He took

158

a swig and swirled it around in his mouth to savor the flavor.

"He said one is Cuban and the other from Texas. I forget which is which," Prince said and took a drink of his own.

"Definitely Cuban. I can taste the safrito!" Angelo said with certainty. They drank their appetizer before hitting the town for another night of debauchery and death. Prince picked out more women to show a good time on the last night of their lives.

The night ended right back where it started and Angelo watched the young buck fuck three more women into submission. It was his own personal porn performance. Then, they dined.

CHAPTER 17

"You look like shit!" Prince said when he found Olivia huddled in a corner of the room. She looked like she just returned from the dead because she did. Now she had a thirst beyond her wildest imagination and she had just imagined some pretty wild stuff.

"What happened to me? I was in hell!" she moaned with the anguish of a person who had seen their reserved spot in the hell fire.

"Yeah, seems that's the downside to this," Prince said with a shrug. He would be stuck with the impetuousness of youth for an eternity. She would find out what was on the other side of the hereafter before he would because her time was up.

Olivia was too shook up to put up much of a fight when Prince attacked. He twisted her head almost completely around with a vicious crunch of bone and cartilage. It wasn't fatal but the wooden stake that followed was. He plunged it into her chest so hard, that the tip came out of her back.

"You're free now," he said since he understood. Not that he believed, so he planned to be the last man standing. Well vampire, man or woman. He felt a boost in power immediately but had no idea what it translated to.

Prince rested for the rest of the day knowing it could be his last. Tonight he would put his plan in motion to secure his future.

When he awoke, his first stop was to the blood bank for a special dinner.

"You can keep the room," Prince told Olivia's shell when he stepped from the shower. It would be his last here since he wasn't coming back. He collected his money from the moneychanger and newest clothes. His new car took him in style over to the blood bank.

Prince drove slowly across town because the ride was so smooth. Plus, he almost feared what lay ahead. He entered the blood bank and headed back to see Charles.

"You're not going to make it," Charles said frankly when he walked in. "I could smell your intentions from the sidewalk. Your thoughts are so loud, I can hear you screaming in my head!"

"I'll be okay," Prince said confidently, so it would be true. He shook his head to clear his thoughts and only hoped it would. "Are you ready?"

"Been ready. Are you? That's the question," he said and retrieved two packets of blood. "Drink. Don't drink."

"Drink, don't drink," Prince repeated and memorized the lot numbers on the bag. He sat them in his bag and stood. There was more in the bag, but he waited for Charles.

Charles stood and spread his fangs one last time. He knew what was coming but couldn't read it from Prince's mind. He nodded, crossed his heart, and stuck his chest out.

Prince pulled the stake from the bag and plunged it deep into his heart. The pleasure prevailed over the pain and spread a smile on his face. Charles's fangs slowly retracted and his eyes blinked death in to view.

"May God forgive me," Charles whispered and there was only one vampire left in the city.

"Good luck with that," Prince said and left the room. He focused his thoughts on a singular pleasure as he drove. The drive was shorter tonight and he arrived at Angelo's sooner than he wanted. He repeated his mantra as he made his way to the door so it would be the only thing on his mind.

"Young Prince," Ralph greeted with a curtsey and let him in.

I want you. I want you, Prince repeated in his head and gave a nod in reply. He followed the man and found Angelo in the study with a young, Latino man on his knees between his legs. His eyes lit up when he saw Prince and what was on his mind.

"Well, it seems like tonight is going to be the start of a new era!" Angelo gushed and batted his eyes. He then snapped the man's neck like a twig since he had no more need for him.

"It is!" Prince said out loud, while still repeating inwardly, I want you. He reached into his bag and produced the packages of blood. Once he saw which one was his, he popped a straw right through the plastic and took a sip.

"Interesting concept?" Angelo said as the juice box was born. "Cool, but it'll never catch on."

"Probably not," Prince agreed and passed him the other packet and a straw. Angelo did what he did and took a sip.

"African?" he suggested of the taste. "Moroccan, I'd say."

I want you. I want you, Prince chanted and sucked down his meal. A slurping sound filled the room once he reached the bottom. He hoped Angelo would follow suit and drain his, as well. He would have if he hadn't felt the affects halfway through.

"What is this?" Angelo asked, feeling weakness overcome him. Ralph went on high alert when he realized the danger.

"Fine silver shavings. Courtesy of Charles who sends his regards once more," Prince said and stood. Silver saps a vampires strength just as kryptonite does people from krypton.

"Why, you—" he said and attempted to stand on wobbly legs. Ralph made the decision to wait for the outcome. To the victor goes the spoils, including him.

Angelo was still a powerful vampire despite losing some strength. He would have still been able to easily kill Prince, had he not added two more fresh kills of his own. Olivia may gave been newly turned, so the gain was nominal. Charles, however, had been around for a century and had plenty of his own powers.

Powers that had now been absorbed by the Dark Prince.

"I want you. I want you to die," Prince repeated and spread his fangs. Both vampires attacked with fangs and claws. Both disappeared and reappeared on opposite sides.

"I've been doing this a hundred years!" Angelo barked and nodded at the gash he carved into Prince's chest.

"You won't be doing it another hundred. You can believe that," Prince snarled and nodded to the similar wound he had inflicted. Both began to close right before their eyes.

The bloody battle waged on blow for bloody blow. It was only Prince's recent increase in power, as well, as the poisonous silver coursing through Angelo's veins that swayed the battle. One last exchange of blows sent Angelo reeling to the floor. Prince pounced with his wooden stake and stood over him.

"Do it!" Angelo demanded defiantly but looked to his help for help. Ralph just turned his head and looked away.

"Consider it done," Prince said and slammed the stake through his chest, heart, and back until it pierced the wooden floor beneath him.

"I am at your service, master," Ralph offered with a bow for good measure.

"Good. Now clean this up," he said, looking down with scorn. "Once you're done I'll hit the town!"

*****

"Save me, Mother Margaret!" a woman pleaded when Prince lowered his fangs towards her juicy jugular vein. Hearing his own mother's name stopped him in his tracks and gave a brief reprieve.

"Who?" he reeled and asked. He listened intently as she explained the patron saint of something. It had been a while since he had been to church and probably would be never before he went again. But the one thing he did remember was that nothing had the right to be worshipped, called upon except God almighty. Alone, with no partners in His Lordship, worship or names and attributes.

"She will save me from you!" she finished. She was suddenly religious, even with a belly and vagina full of vampire come.

"Well, how long 'til she gets here?" Prince asked sarcastically. He was going to hell anyway, so why not make fun of all things holy?

"Huh?" the woman asked like she never thought of that. She was a party girl and just wanted to party. The rich, tall, dark, and handsome Prince swept her off her feet and into his bed. She saved nothing for marriage and let him in every hole in her body. Now three inch fangs came out trying to make a few more holes in her body.

"Nothing," he shrugged and bit her. He held her tight as a grandmother's hug as he drained her blood and life from her body. "Prince, a hundred. God, zero."

Hearing his mother's name reminded him of his promise and mission in Atlanta. He loved this new city but, a promise is a promise, especially when it's to your mother.

"Ralph!" Prince called to summon his helper. Ralph was actually working out pretty well since he knew the city like the back of his hand. He was able to transfer all of Angelo's property into his name and made him rich. Prince didn't need the house in Atlanta, he wanted it.

"Yes, Master Prince?" Ralph announced upon arrival. He saw the fresh corpse and moved to clean the room. Living in South Florida meant plenty of hungry alligators to take care of the leftovers.

"Handle this, then pack my bags," he said and went to shower the sex and blood away. Both set off on their missions and met back in the study.

"Shall I pack a bag and come with you?" Ralph asked eagerly.

"No. I have another thing you can help me with," he said and passed him a glass of red wine. They toasted and tossed back their drinks.

"No!" Ralph pleaded when the taste of blood registered.

"Pretty much," Prince nodded. "There's a vampire in Atlanta already and I must have the upper hand."

"But, but I..." he was trying to explain but death interrupted before he could finish.

"See you in a few," Prince said and retired to his bedroom. When he awoke later that afternoon, he would have a vampire to kill. It would add to his strength for the trip to Atlanta.

CHAPTER 18

Prince felt like a new vampire after he took Ralph's life the next afternoon. That meant he had to drive himself to Atlanta because they didn't have "colored" airplanes yet. The bus did but would have exposed him to the deadly sunlight. He had plenty of powers that he usurped from his vampire victims but daywalker was not one of them. It was the goal and he planned to keep killing until he reached it. That meant whoever this Daryl in Atlanta was, was in trouble.

Prince drove the comfortable Caddie through the night until the approach of dawn. He was lucky to find a colored motor lodge near Jacksonville and rented a room. It may have been coloreds only but that didn't stop white men from swinging by for some brown sugar.

He rested until dusk and hit the road once more. There were a few hours of darkness left when he pulled into the city of Atlanta. A strange feeling engulfed him when he saw the familiar sights of his youth. There's no place like home and the Dark Prince was home.

"Let's see how the old house is holding up," he said aloud as he navigated to his old neighborhood. Luckily, it was dark enough that everyone couldn't see the young black man driving a new Cadillac in this part of town.

The old house hadn't changed much, but he noticed the differences. His doting dad would never let the grass get that long and the hedges weren't even. No, this wouldn't do at all, so he would just take the house back.

"Uh oh," Prince mused when a patrol car jumped behind him.

"What's this nigga doing over here?" the driver of the cop car wanted to know.

"Come for some white girl, I betcha," his partner surmised and lit up his lights.

"Dinner is served!" Prince smiled and pulled over to the curb. He rolled down his window and waited for them to approach.

"License and registration," the first one demanded, while the second one was ready to shoot him when he reached for it.

"I don't have any of that stuff," Prince said dismissively. He added sarcastic smirk to speed things along.

"Here for some white girl, aren't you?" the second asked.

"Yup. Gonna feed her this big black dick until she chokes. Then take her over to the trap and pimp her for a dollar."

"Get yo black ass out of the car!" the driver demanded and snatched him out. He saw his partner lift his walkie-talkie and quickly shut him down. "No! Don't call this in. He's going to the Woodlawn precinct."

"Ah yeah, Woodlawn!" his partner laughed. Many a belligerent black man ended up in the Woodlawn precinct. The name Woodlawn cemetery was more fitting because if they die they die.

169

Prince hummed a happy tune as they rode along the darkened Atlanta streets. Memories of happier times flooded his mind as the scenery passed by the window.

"Hey, this doesn't look like a precinct to me?" Prince said with mock concern. He was actually elated when they pulled to a deserted corner and pulled him from the car.

"You like white girls, huh?" the cop snarled and took a swing at his handcuffed prisoner. Prince opened wide and his whole hand ended up in his mouth. He bit down and took his hand off at the wrist.

"What the—" the second cop asked in disbelief. He shook his head to reset his vision because surely he did not see what he just saw.

"Fuck?" Prince asked to be helpful and snapped the cuffs like they were made of paper.

The screaming cop annoyed him, so he took a swipe with his claws and decapitated him. That was all the other needed to see before he pulled his gun. His quickly emptied the six shot revolver but kept pulling the trigger since the man was still standing.

"Who are you!" the cop shouted. He had shot quite a few black men before and none took six shots standing. He usually had to empty his gun on them while they were on the ground.

"What am I, is a better question," Prince corrected before he pounced. He pulled the man's head back so hard, the crack of bones sent sleeping birds fluttering from the trees. He bit away a huge chunk of the cop's neck and caused blood to spew from the wound. It reminded him of drinking from the garden hose when he fed. He drank his fill and left the police right there where they lay.

Prince found a colored motel and rented a room for a week. That's how long he gave himself to take back what belonged to him.

*****

"Hmph," Mr. King said when he felt that strange feeling of someone watching him. It could have been because he knew he was wrong by creeping away at night while his wife slept. He had a penchant for black vagina and couldn't get that at home.

At least he thought she was sleep because she turned a blind eye to his extra curricular sexual activities. She was a freak herself and would gladly do all the freaky things he got from across the tracks, but he preferred to go across the tracks anyway.

Prince ran along side of his car in a black blur until he selected a black whore for the evening. Once he knew he would be preoccupied, he rushed back to the man's house. The black blur went unnoticed in the white neighborhood and he entered the King family home through the back door.

"Well, that was quick," Mrs. King said to herself when she heard the creaking of her creaky steps. She was glad her husband never fixed it since it gave her a warning when he was coming. Plenty enough time to stop playing in her pussy for the satisfaction he was lacking.

She closed her eyes and leaned her head to the side like she would for her husband to slip in beside her. Some nights she could smell the sex on his breath and hands. This night he just stood in the doorway and stared. Had it been a staring contest, she would have lost because she opened one lid for a peep.

"Ah!" Mrs. King gasped when she saw the tall, dark figure in her doorway. He was completely naked, so she knew what he was after. Still she didn't scream. Her pussy was still soaking wet and throbbing from being interrupted.

"Take the cover away," Prince said in his hypnotic voice. He wasn't quite sure if it worked yet or not, but she did complied. Now he was sure it didn't work when she reached her hand back between her legs and began to rub. His dick throbbed to a full erection as he neared. He didn't want to interrupt her again, so he pushed inside of her mouth.

Prince stroked her mouth like it was a vagina while she played in her pussy. Had this been a race it would have been declared a tie because an orgasm shook her soul as he filled her mouth.

"On your stomach," he demanded and she flipped over and arched her back. Her pink pussy poked out from the white cheeks like a bulls eye.

She was so wet, Prince just plunged inside and sank to the bottom. A place where her husband had never been. She stretched out, gripped the sheets and arched her back even more so he could get every nook and cranny. He got every nook and cranny, too, and fucked the daylights out of her.

Mrs. King came so many times, she almost passed out from the pleasure. Prince could have gone all night but knew her husband couldn't. By his observation, the man was on the way home right now. He sped up and filled the tight box full of vampire cum.

"Now, get your husband's books. Bring them to me," Prince directed. Again, he wasn't sure if it was his power of hypnosis or the fact that good dick makes things happen. Whichever it was, the woman dipped into the closet and came up with the second set of books the man kept.

"Here you are," she said and handed them over with a curtsey. "Will you cum back?"

"Hop on one leg and bark!" he ordered.

"Why?" Mrs. King asked as she lifted one leg to do what he said.

"Never mind," Prince sighed when he realized it was the good dick and not hypnosis. The pussy was good though, so he answered. "Of course!"

*****

173

"Gotcha!" Prince cheered when he reviewed the documents. His plan to murder the man went out the window when he saw how much dirt he had done. Death was too good and too easy. He would destroy him instead. Then kill him.

"Should have kept Ralph," he mused since he needed someone to do his bidding. All vampires kept a pet to do odd jobs for them. He stepped out of his room to recruit one, but a commotion caught his attention. A slowly moving procession moved up the street behind a man preaching through a bullhorn.

"All men were created equal and we will not rest until all men are treated equal!" he said and got back a chorus of "amens" and "mmhm" in reply.

"Who was that?" Prince asked one of the working girls who worked the hotel.

"Dr. Martin Luther King!" she said loud and proud. Prince knew he must have been somebody to make a working girl stick out her chest in pride instead of to attract a trick. This was the midst of the civil rights movement and the Dark Prince was right there.

He felt another strong presence along with the larger than life presence of the pragmatic preacher. The deacon beside Dr. King felt it too and turned to see where it came from. The two vampires locked eyes for the first time but knew it wouldn't be the last. He picked up one of the pamphlets being passed out and saw the Ebenezer Baptist Church promoting night services by Deacon Daryl Davis. Prince had just found Daryl and visa versa.

The moment passed and he took the hooker in his room and fucked the daylights out of her until daylight. He paid her for her pussy then a little more for a little more of her time. She did his ripping and running and set his plans in motion.

*****

"It's me, Andrea!" the hooker called as she knocked on the motel door. She had done what she was asked and wanted to get paid for it. This was money she wouldn't have to turn in to her pimp since he didn't know about it yet. Not yet anyway because one of her sister whores seen her enter the room and planned to report it. There's no honor amongst thieves and even less between prostitutes.

"What did you find out?" he asked as she came in and closed the door behind her.

"First of all, it's too damn dark in here!" she protested and tried to open the curtain. Prince moved across the room with super human speed before she could. Her eyes went wide with shock at the sight.

"I like it dark," he shrugged as that explained what she just saw. "What did you find?"

"Oh, um. Okay," she stammered and caught her bearings. She knew a porter at the courthouse and was able to find out that Mr. King, unlike Dr. King, was a thief. He pulled all kinds of schemes to take black peoples' money and houses.

"Hmph," he said when he saw this courthouse records didn't match up with the books he got from his wife. The thought of the sex with the sexy white woman made him grow stiff in his underwear.

"Need me to take care of that?" she asked when she saw the movement in his drawers.

"No, I'm good," he said since he decided to see Mrs. King again tonight. Besides, the wheels turning in his head required some quiet time to think. He dismissed her with her pay and sent her away. Well, tried to anyway.

"Un huh!" Andrea's pimp shouted and delivered a back hand, pimp slapping her the second she stepped from the room. Prince's fangs slid out in anticipation for battle.

"Here! Here!" Andrea pleaded and handed him the money she just made. It was enough to satisfy him but he still knocked on the door to see who was spending so well. He would much rather take it all at one time instead of a trickle from him tricking.

"I'm sleep now. Can you come back tonight?" Prince asked through the door.

"I'll be back nigga!" the pimp fussed and stomped off. Either way, his stay there had come to an end. He had staked out a similar spot not too far just in case, and just in case just came knocking.

CHAPTER 19

Prince walked into the historic church and felt a shiver go through his spine. He grew up in churches like this but now felt no attachment to the God the preacher was preaching about. Hell was his destination and he accepted it. Now the question was, why was a vampire preaching about salvation?

Daryl acknowledged Prince's presence with the slightest of pauses and kept on preaching. Prince found a seat in the rear and sent telepathic messages, but Daryl never looked up. He knew then that he wasn't powerful enough to read minds.

He could only hope he would be after dispatching the two new vampires he had brewing back at the motel. The pimp came back as promised but it didn't work out quite according to his plans. Now he and Andrea were somewhere between life and death as they turned from human to vampire. Once their transformation was complete, they would add to Prince's collection of kills.

"Did you enjoy the service?" Daryl asked as he slid next to his new friend.

"Huh?" Prince asked and looked around the nearly deserted church. He had zoned out and missed most of the message. It would have been wasted on him anyway since his desires were his new god. God said whoever followed their desires as their god, would end up in hell.

"I see. Anyway, let's go somewhere and talk," Daryl said and stood. It was more like an order since he wanted to get the vampire away from the congregation. It took decades before he could handle all the bearing hearts thundering in his ears. The smell of menses wafting in the air from several sources of women and teen girls used to drive him crazy. Dr. King had nicked himself real good one time while shaving and almost changed the history books.

"Yeah," Prince agreed before someone got eaten. He nodded in agreement again at the nearly new Cadillac Daryl drove. "The word pays well, I see."

"Not for me. This came courtesy of a blood donor," he explained.

"So, how exactly does drinking blood and preaching coexist in the same frame?" Prince wanted to know. It seemed incongruent at best in his amateur eyes.

"God is real and we, our kind, are really doomed to the fire," he laid out much as a construction worker does a foundation. Once it was set, he could build upon it.

"If you say so," he said since he no longer believed. He traded his hereafter for here and now when he begged Katrina to turn him.

"I say so. There's some bad, really bad people in this world. In this city, drinking their blood is a public service," Daryl said as he drove. "Pimps, pushers, child molesters and such. They taste so sweet."

"I take it we're about to find out," Prince said as they crept into a rundown section of the city.

"We are. Tell me if you see something you like," Daryl said. He spotted a dealer he'd been wanting to drink from but let his guest pick.

"There!" Prince said and pointed as a cop took a woman behind the building. They parked and went around behind them.

"That's it, you black whore!" the cop said as he humped her face.

"You're giving instructions like you sucked a dick before!" Daryl said as they approached.

"Deacon Davis!" Prince mocked in feigned shock. That got a pretty good laugh out of both men, but the cop didn't think it was so funny. Especially in the middle of his break.

"Tell you what boy..." he barked and paused to let the slander sink in. "If y'all don't get y'all black asses away from here rat now, y'all finna take her place!"

"Okay," Prince said and dismissed the girl. The cop pulled his gun but the vampires drew their fangs. The cop wasn't able to get off a shot or let out a scream before he had a vampire latched on to both sides of his neck. They drained him dry in seconds and let him crumple to the concrete below. The men would feed on two more death deserving people before dawn began to creep.

"We must do this again?" Daryl asked hopefully. He loved spreading the word of God, but he still had to eat.

"We shall, and soon," Prince assured him as they separated. He, too, enjoyed the company but still, there could be only one.

*****

"What goes around comes back around again," Prince gloated when the insurance and bank scandal came down. So many powerful people had their greedy hands in the mix, they simply reversed their thievery, and returned properties back to whom they belonged. Prince got his family home back but wasn't finished with Mr. King. A quick death was far too humane for this monster. He was going to really make him suffer.

He watched and waited for him drive away in search of some brown sugar despite having a perfectly good pussy at home. It was so good, Prince made sure to come get some every time Mr. King left the house.

"I've been, ssss, waiting on you!" Mrs. King hissed and made herself cum with her fingers. She had been playing in it from the second her husband left the house but seeing Prince appear in her doorway sent her over the edge.

"You've been waiting for this," he corrected and whipped out the wood. He walked over and dropped it right into her mouth. Her head bobbed feverishly but he was in no hurry tonight. No tonight, he wanted to get caught. He took his time and got completely naked and stretched out on the bed.

They flipped around into a figure 69 and pleasured each other simultaneously. Prince heard Mr. King when he pulled up, but Mrs. King didn't hear him until he reached that creaky step. There was time aplenty to get that dick out her mouth but she didn't.

Mr. King crept into the bedroom and paused in his tracks. He blinked, rubbed his eyes, and blinked again but some black man was still fucking his wife's face. He turned the light on, but that only made it worse.

"What in Sam Hill is going on here!" he demanded. His wife could only gag, so Prince spoke for the both of them.

"Get your gun," he ordered and the man turned like a zombie to comply. His latest conquest granted him the power to make mortals do whatever he told them. "Now watch."

Mr. King was totally coherent but unable to move or even look away while Prince literally fucked the dog shit out of his wife. The woman howled like a wolf as he stroked her to orgasm after orgasm. He was almost impressed at how much dick she could take and how limber she was. Prince had her practically folded in half with her feet behind her ears as he delivered the dick.

"The show is just about—" he said and scrambled to pull out and reach her mouth. He exploded on her face and shoved himself inside her mouth. "Over! Whew! And you leave this for street whores?"

"I..." Mr. King said and realized he had regained control over himself. He quickly raised the gun and pumped three rounds into the adulterer and adulteress. They both slumped over dead on the spot.

He went back downstairs to fix a stiff drink and call police. His story would be that he found an intruder fucking his wife and killed him. She was a casualty he could live with since she enjoyed it so much. The police moved pretty quickly in the white neighborhoods, so he had to slam his glass back to finish his drink when they pulled up.

"Where is he?" a police officer asked as he came in with his gun drawn. He could only pray this black intruder still had a breath in him so he could finish him off.

"Upstairs. In my bed!" he said and pointed the way. The first two cops rushed up the stairs and into the room. They came down two minutes wearing mask of confusion just as other units arrived on the scene.

"What'll we got?" the sergeant asked when he came in. The cops whispered something in his ear and he rushed up the stairs, too. He, too, came back minutes later with that same mask on. "Mr. King, tell me what happened here tonight.

"I came home and Sarah was screaming and I, and he was," he stammered, rambling through his lie. "So I shot him. I accidentally may have hit her, too," he repeated as rehearsed.

"Show me what you mean," the sergeant asked. He fell in step behind Mr. King and headed into the bedroom.

"But, he, and I—how?" he stammered once more when he only found his dead wife alone in the bed. That was good for a death sentence just like his actions got for Prince's mother.

CHAPTER 20

Prince and Deacon Daryl had become thick as thieves. They got together almost every night and fed off the cities undesirables. The two vampires literally took a bite out of crime. Crime rates actually went down in some areas when people started coming up missing.

Prince even traveled with the freedom fighters to different southern cities. Anytime the local racists and racist cops would abuse Dr. King or any of his people, Prince and Daryl would eat them once the sunset.

Thursday night, April 4th,1968, they were in Memphis, Tennessee at the Lorraine motel. Prince was enjoying some good Memphis pussy when a single shot rang out and changed history. The world as well as his. He heard the commotion and Andrew Young clearly say, "They shot Martin".

"Aaaah!" the woman he was with screeched when his fangs popped out. His hand tightened around her throat to shut her up and shut her up for good. The meal went to waste because he'd lost his appetite.

To make matters worse, he and Daryl couldn't join the men on the balcony and missed being a part of that famous picture pointing to where the shot came from. He could only pace the room until the second the sun lowered under the horizon. Both, he and Daryl, bolted out of their rooms but missed all the action. This was the south, during the civil

184

rights movement, so there was plenty action to be found.

A Klan rally just happened to rally right by the motel. The two vampires looked at each other and bared their fangs in a wicked smile. They were a blur as they trailed the hundred white men in white robes out to a field. A large wooden cross was soaked in kerosene for what was supposed to be the main event. Except now, the itinerary had just been changed.

A speaker took to the pulpit to espouse some racist bullshit but wouldn't get his point across tonight. Prince and Daryl attacked from both ends and the KKK didn't stand a chance. Hair, skin, and blood flew through the night as they savagely ravaged the men who liked to call other men boys, yet screamed like girls.

The vampires were a black blur as white robes turned red and racist lay dead. In a matter of minutes, it looked like a field had been mowed clean as the men lay in pieces.

"Our work here is done," Daryl said with a satisfied smirk as he surveyed the damaged.

"Not quite," Prince said and struck once more. He caught his friend off guard and quickly nailed him to the cross.

"What are you doing?" Daryl asked in confusion. They had been friends for a year and he assumed they were past this.

"There can be only one," he said almost sadly and used one of the dead racist's lighters to light the cross. Daryl could have broken free but chose a chance at salvation. He lifted his head proudly and let the fire consume him. Now, he was free.

*****

Prince was lonely in Atlanta without his friend. Ironic since he was the one who killed him. He took solace in the power he absorbed from yet another kill. He now could turn invisible to mortals on command. He still wanted to read minds, shift shapes and fly like a bat. He would need more vampires for that. Turning new ones was slow going and not enough power for a power drunk, young vampire. He was in a rut but it took fifteen years before he decided to do something.

"Time to take my show on the road?" Prince asked aloud and answered with a nod. He travelled north by night to Charlotte, North Carolina and checked into a room.

The civil rights movement paid dividends and motels were no longer segregated. Especially the truck stops with disposable people to feed on and transients who would not be missed. Most had drug and alcohol problems which gave their blood an odd taste. Food was food, so he dined nonetheless.

He was dining on a lounge lizard when he felt the presence of one of his own. His head snapped up just in time to see another vampire attack. The large white trucker swung a sword that nearly ended Prince's story early. The woman he was dining on rolled away and ran off as the men squared off for battle. Blood skeeted from the two holes in her jugular veins with every beat of her heart. She didn't make it far until she ran out of gas and keeled over dead.

"Just give it up, boy!" the trucker suggested and took another swipe. Prince smiled when he felt the man's fear. He was living as a truck driver to stay two steps ahead of other vampires. Plus, he was able to spread his carnage around the country so he wouldn't bring too much attention to himself.

"Give up my head? You may as well chop your own head off," Prince laughed and bared his claws. He dipped and ducked his swipes and pokes of the sword, while slashing the mans' face and chest. The wounds closed immediately after opening.

"Looks like a draw," the trucker said once the battle got them no where. Not to mention people were starting to gather to watch. He lowered his sword and Prince raised his hands in surrender.

"Or not!" Prince laughed and cut the man's head off with his claws. The small crowd screamed and took off running for their lives. Prince had only been in town one day and wore out his welcome. The upside was another vampire was under his belt and he felt a surge in power. It was time to move on, so he moved north by night until he reached New York City.

It was the beginning of the rap music era and Prince loved it. The late nights, the music, drugs, sordid sex and debauchery was right up his alley. He immersed himself in the culture and hung out with the elite rappers as a part of their entourage. He can still be seen in early pictures with LL Cool J, Run Dmc and others.

The life of excess, extras and etceteras were right up his alley. The lights, camera and action of the nightlife suited him just fine. The rappers lived by night and slept by day just like he did. They bedded different women at night and disposed of them in the morning, just like he did. Being a rapper was just like being a vampire, so why not be both?

Being forever young has obvious advantages but disadvantages, as well. Prince stayed the same age while everyone around him aged. Love wasn't an option for him. He found that out the hard way after falling hard for a beautiful Dominican groupie. They dated for months until one morning he awoke to find her lifeless and drained of all of her blood. Had he had a heart, it would have been broken. He didn't, so he just got angry. Love reminded him of his mother, father, grandmother, and Antoinette.

Prince fit right in with the lavish lifestyle of the rich and famous. He drank and smoked to excess with the excessive people, even though neither affected him. He could only be young for so long, so twenty years later, he moved on.

*****

Prince's next stop was Los Angeles, California. The bloody gang wars were right up his alley. It allowed him to feed with impunity since the murder rate was so high. They also had a vibrant rap scene and he slid right in. He fed off groupies and street thugs just like he had in Atlanta and New York.

"Prince, my man!" a rapper named Butta shouted and stood to give him a pound when he arrived in the nightclub.

"What's up, homie?" he greeted with a pound and man hug. The two had gotten close during a recent tour and hung out quite often.

"My video shoot in the morning! You coming?" he asked hopefully. Prince wasn't the average hanger on since he was rich himself. In fact, his good looks, and dark demeanor put him in high demand. Actually, he was the man. No one knew exactly what he did but it obviously paid well. Well enough to invest in movies and music to make more money.

"Morning? I don't do mornings," Prince dismissed with a wave of his diamond laden hand.

"Nah, you don't. What are you, a vampire or something?" the rapper joked and laughed.

"Actually, I am," Prince said and wiped the smile off his face. Little did he know the man had been wondering that for some time. Like Prince in his youth, Butta, too, was a vampire buff. He read all the books and watched all the movies.

"Man, that's so cool! Do me! Turn me? Please!" he begged and pleaded. Prince actually thought about it for a moment. On one hand, it would be cool to have a companion but there was still that other hand. The one that would one day take his life and power. "Yo, I always wanted to be a vampire! I seen all the movies! Read all the books! I—"

"I'm kidding! Look at your face, yo! You really believe in vampires? Bruh, there's no such thing as vampires," Prince assured him and laughed. He laughed so heartily, the man backtracked and shook his head.

"I was kidding, too! Man, ain't no such a thing!" Butta said and twisted his lips. The moment passed but not his suspicion. He knew a vampire when he saw one and this dude was a vampire. "So look, the video last all damn day ,so swing through later. At night?"

"Bet that," Prince agreed and scanned the club for a desert and dinner. A woman to enjoy before and after to fuck and suck.

"Looks like you got a fish on a your hook," his friend said of the woman who stared up at Prince from the dance floor. She turned around to show him what she was working with and got her man.

"Indeed, I do," he said and gravitated to the dance floor.

"Make sure to let her ride backwards!" he said. He would know since she rode him backwards on quite a few occasions.

"Come," Prince said in passing and the woman dropped everything and everyone and followed him out of the club.

"He definitely a vampire," Butta said when he saw how easily he scooped Yasmine from the club. It took him months and thousands to get her to mount his horsey and ride it backwards. Prince had the power of hypnosis but didn't use it because he didn't need it.

"I was wondering when you were going to get around to me," Yasmine said when he lifted the Lexus door to help her inside.

"Damn, me too!" Prince said when she spread her legs as she was seated in the car. Her kitty was shaved to show off how plump and pretty it was. He made the decision to eat her before he drank her.

"Careful, she bites. Grrr!" Yasmine teased and giggled.

"So do I," Prince laughed. He didn't return the growl since he growled for real. Lexus's are built for speed, not blowjobs, so he had to wait until they reached his beachfront home. Being on the west coast allowed him to see the inviting sunsets instead of the dangerous sunrises, UV tinted windows protecting him from the rays.

"Nice place," Yasmine said just like all the others. Soon she would be fucked, sucked and tossed in the beautiful Pacific ocean to feed the sharks, just like all the others.

191

"Thanks. Now I'm tryna see your place," he said as he led her into his bedroom. They were there to fuck, so they skipped the small talk and stripped. Both was equally impressed by the other's nakedness. He won when his dick seemed to rise on command right before her eyes.

"Top or bottom?" Yasmine asked as they mounted the California king sized bed.

"Um..." he paused to think. Position plays an important role in a good 69. Being on the bottom gives a woman space to work her head game so he said, "You can get the top."

The couple arranged themselves for mutual oral combat and set out to please each other. The battle wouldn't be quite fair since Prince had extraordinary speed. He flicked his tongue feverishly until she released a nut on his chin. Once she recovered, she returned the favor and received a mouthful of appreciation.

They switched positions so she could lay on her back. Prince took position between her legs so he could deliver the dick. He took his time to admire her pretty face, fat breasts, and hard stomach. He rubbed his dick between her slippery pussy lips then squinted at the faint line above her pubic mound. The remnants of a C-section from a quality surgeon.

"That's where my little man came out, so mommy's coochie can stay nice and tight," Yasmine explained when she realized what he was looking at. Little did she know she had just saved her own life. He spared mothers when they were being mothers.

"You'll have to thank him for me," Prince chuckled and slid into that tight pussy. It was so tight, it took the smile right off of his face. Hers, too, when he began to stroke her to orgasm after orgasm until she tapped out. He ended hours later by skeeting on the C-section scar.

She curled up into a fetal ball and he rolled off his bed. There would be no drinking straight from the tap tonight, so he entered his kitchen and opened the fridge. Old Charles from Miami crossed his mind and left a smile on his face when he saw the packs of plasma. He selected one and sank his fangs inside.

Prince drank his fill before summoning a car service to take his guest home. Getting put out after sex sure beat being drained dry and tossed in the ocean, but Yasmine still had an attitude. She would never know how close she came to the end of her life.

This was life until he got too old to still be so young. It was almost another twenty years before it was time to move on. Prince selected a city with both a vibrant hip-hop scene as well as a high murder rate. One such city fit the bill on both categories.

The Dark Prince was headed back to Atlanta.

CHAPTER 21

"Welcome to Atlanta," Prince said to himself when his plane began to descend on the darkened city. He never liked flying since all the heartbeats contained in the small space almost drove him to drink. Blood, not vodicka.

Prince tried to ignore his thirst as he made his way through the crowded airport. He could hear blood coursing through the people around him as the tram made its way to the baggage claim. A woman on her period posted up next him and smiled flirtatiously up at him.

"Well, hello," she offered along with anything that came of it.

"Mmph," he grunted dismissively to save her from him.

"What a waste," she said and shook her head. Atlanta is the gayest city in America, so she assumed he was one of them. So did the gay guy who had his eyes on Prince since he boarded. He assumed the same when he saw the snub. Gay or not, even he recognized that was a bad chick who just got dissed.

"Hey," the man said and made his move. "Visiting or coming home? Business or pleasure?"

"Coming home and it is a pleasure," Prince replied. The woman scoffed and pushed off with her head high. She'd already lost a husband to a man and now this fine man chose a man over her. She was one step closer to being a lesbian.

"I'm Aaron. Can I buy you a drink?" the man offered and peered into his dark eyes to convey the rest of the invitation.

"I'd rather drink you," Prince whispered. An hour later, they reached the man's midtown condo. It was well appointed and clean like a woman lived there. Was, since it was about to be a crime scene. Dawn was close, so there wasn't much time to waste.

"Welcome," the man said and stepped aside to let his guest enter. "Can I get you anything?"

"A sharp knife," Prince commanded. Aaron didn't understand the command but rushed to carry it out. He entered his kitchen and selected a knife from his expensive set.

"Cut both of your wrist. Deep," Prince ordered and moved in for a drink. The man could only watch as his life liquid leaked from one wrist while being drained from the other.

Prince learned from trial and error how to clean up his messes. Leaving empty corpses behind was a magnet for other vampires as well as vampire hunters, do-gooders who tracked down and killed his kind on sight. He drank his fill and left the rest to make it look like a suicide.

*****

"Well, this is a first," the nosey installer said once he wrapped up an odd request for a side job. His greed got him talked into installing a mini crematorium in Prince's basement.

195

"A last, as well," Prince replied. "Now, show me again how it works."

"Depends on what you tryna burn. This baby will take a two hundred pound man down to ash in minutes! What you say you was tryna burn?" he inquired again as he ran him through the operating procedures.

"How much did you say you weighed?" he asked in reply to his question.

"About two hundred," the man nodded. It would be his last nod because Prince latched onto his neck and bit down. He put up a good fight until there wasn't enough blood to power his muscles to fight with. His body went limp when Prince reached the bottom with a loud slurp like the end of a soft drink.

"Okay. Now, you said..." Prince said as he duplicated the steps to operate the machine. He placed the body inside and sure enough, it was reduced to ash in a matter of minutes.

It had been almost fifty years, so Prince did some Internet shopping to update his home. The city's swank malls were open late allowing him to update his wardrobe as well.

"Are you sure?" he asked when the sales girl showed him the latest fashions for men. They seemed to look a lot like the latest fashion for women.

"Of course, I'm sure..." she said and paused, whipping out her phone. She scrolled her IG and verified that men now dressed like girls. "Try them on and see how you look in the mirror."

"Is there a middle course?" he asked since he didn't do mirrors and mirrors didn't do him. He was quite pleased to find some jeans and slacks that didn't hug his nuts like an anaconda.

"Is that all?" she asked flirtatiously but Prince didn't take the bait. He tried to spare people who would be missed and this girl would be missed.

"That's all," he declined since he was more hungry than horny. She poked her bottom lip out in a pout as he walked out of her store and life.

*****

Prince had a couple of cars but liked to travel by train and bus. It allowed him to pick up strays and runaways. The ones who wouldn't be missed.

"Yup, there she is," Prince said when a young began to twerk for no other reason than to get his intention. She got it, too, but that wasn't a good thing.

"Sup, shawty?" the girl almost dared when she approached him. The armful of bags worked more than his good looks.

"You," he smiled, then laughed since he didn't have to use his hypnotic powers. He hardly got to use them when it came to women. Sometimes he would just sing and they would flock around. A week ago, he gorged himself on four friends who loved his singing.

197

"You ain't tryna fuck nothing?" she offered with her hands on her hips as advertisement. He ran his legs up her exposed legs and the short, shorts pulled snugly into her crotch. That was advertising, as well.

"Let me see what you working with." Prince said and turned her to the side. He was quite impressed with the roundness of her ass and sealed the deal along with her fate. They rode a few more stops before Prince led her away.

"Why you on the train if you got a car?" she squealed when they got off the train and hit the parking lot.

"So I could meet you," he said truthfully. He didn't tell her the rest or she would have ran for her life. Instead, she rode to her death.

"Who stay here?" lil' mama asked when Prince escorted her inside of his house and up to his room.

"Just me," he said and disrobed. She followed suit and joined him on the bed. Now it was his turn to be surprised at how worn out the young girl's vagina was. It had more miles on it than a Marta bus and smelled similar.

Prince could usually go for hours but decided to cut it short. He stroked her to her first orgasm as a going away present before biting her neck. His crematory made quick work of the girl in minutes. The night was still young, so he decided to head out for seconds.

*****

"Jeff said he can put you on nights. Just a couple nights a week," Angela said hopefully. She could only hope her baby daddy, Demetrious, would take it and take some of the load off of her back.

"Nights? Why not days with you? You know I need to be out scouting for talent at night!" he whined. He would work odd jobs when he had to, but he dreamed of being a music manager and living the good life.

"I'on know, Meech," Angela lied. A slight, white lie since she didn't want to admit her boss was trying to fuck her. She flirted back, a little in exchange for as many hours as she could handle. The woman would never cheat but the family had to eat. Besides, she believed in her man and knew he would make it happen.

"Man, I'm right there, too! I got these girls who can be the next TLC!" he vowed. That didn't make it quite true either. While the girls could sing, they were ugly and no label wants an ugly R and B group. The TLC in this case stood for, "they look crazy". They should be called CBA for cockeyed, bucktooth and acne. It would certainly have fit better.

"Hmph! Like I said, a few nights a week," she huffed since she saw the girls.

"Give me a week. If I can't get them signed in a week, then I'm coming to work with y'all," he acquiesced.

"Well, you ain't getting no pussy 'til you either got a deal or a job," she giggled. They both knew that was a lie since the cute, squat couple was hopelessly in love. The little girl sleeping in her crib was a testament of that love.

"Well, I'm finna hit the club, so—" was all he was able to get out before she attacked.

Demetrious wasn't the most handsome man in the city, but he was hers. No way was she letting him to go into one of these clubs unfucked. She reasoned he wouldn't need no pussy if he just got some pussy . They made love face to face in a quick but mutually satisfying session. He showered, dressed, and headed out into the night.

"Shit! Shit, shit, shit!" he fussed when their car wouldn't start. He didn't know anything about cars but still lifted the hood to see what was wrong. He didn't, so he rushed out to the bus stop so he wouldn't miss the showcase.

Demetrious was sure he could make it since his cousin, Dirt, was the hottest rapper in the city right now. They came up like brothers in their grandmother's house on the west side. They even formed a rap group dubbed Dirt Jones and Lil Meech. Dirt got noticed one night when Meech couldn't get out and never looked back. Demetrious settled on being a manager, now all he needed was an act.

"Tosha. My car died, so just meet me at the club," he directed and hung up before she could ask how they were supposed to get there since he was supposed to pick them up.

*****

"There he go!" Tosha pointed when Meech arrived at the club. He was out of shape, so the few blocks from the train to the club left him out of breath. He was happy to see his girls but not the unhappy looking taxi driver.

"They said you paying for the ride!" he asked with an exclamation point since it wasn't a question.

"Um, yeah. How much?" he asked and pulled out his last twenty dollar bill.

"Nineteen dollars and seventy five cents," he said and pointed at his meter to prove it. Meech wanted to cry when he turned over his last. It was the whole allowance Angela allowed him to keep in his pocket.

"Let me get my quarter!" Meech whined.

"Quick playing!" Tosha insisted and pulled him away, while pus oozed from a pimple she popped earlier.

"Come on. Y'all look..." he said, looking for a compliment but didn't find one. So he shrugged and led the way to the entrance.

"Look what?" Kamala asked, looking at him with one eye and the other across the street. She didn't get many compliments, so she wanted to hear it.

"We wook wood!" Kelli declared for them. Her buckteeth turned a lot of letters into Ws when she spoke, but she could sing her flat ass off.

"Yeah, you do," he said even though they didn't. That's why he had a plan to get

201

around their looks. Their voices should be all that matters anyway.

"Psssh," the bouncer huffed when he saw Meech and company. He didn't think much of him but had orders to let him in.

"They with me," he said of the girls behind him like he was a somebody. The bouncer "pssshed" once more and let them in.

"We in!" Kamala cheered, looking at the stage and VIP section simultaneously.

"Okay, look. Here's the plan..." Meech said once they got backstage. He set them up with their mics and went to VIP to find his cousin.

"You know you can't come up in here!" the large man told Meech when he reached the velvet rope separating regular people from the so-called very important people. Oddly enough, there wasn't a single teacher, preacher, or Imam in there, so it was unclear what made them so very important.

"Let him in," Dirt said despite having told him not to let his cousin in.

"Told you!" Meech bucked up at the big man, then cowered under his glare. "Sup, cuz!"

"Mmhm," Dirt said, ignoring his outstretched hand. Meech just gave himself five and continued.

"These chicks are it! They hot! Hot, I tell you!" he vowed.

"Bruh, this the ATL. Bad bitches is a dime a dozen. Can they sing? We need us a dope R and B group," he said. Every rapper wants a label and every label needs an R and B group.

"They can sing!" Meech repeated and they were on the verge of finding out. "We finna get this showcase started!" The DJ announced and cut the music. He was instructed to let Meech's group go first so they could get out the way.

"First up. T.K.K?"

"We working on the name," Meech answered the "wtf" on his cousin's face on hearing the name. "Cuz, they like the next TLC! Well, you can name them once you sign them."

"Mmhm," Dirt hummed skeptically. His face changed when the girls began harmonizing acapella off stage. Meech smiled so wide, his cheeks hurt when he saw his cousin perk up and pop up from his chair.

The girls launched into a medley of TLC classics, minus the music to show their range. They took turns with lead while harmonizing the background. Keli even rapped the late great Left Eye's parts. They weren't halfway through when Dirt made up his mind to sign them on the spot. He planned to smash too because what's the sense of having an R and B group if you're not fucking them.

"Go get em! Cuz, you in. Go get em!" Dirt demanded the second they wrapped up their set. The mystery of not seeing the girls, singing off stage had the whole club intrigued.

"Yes!" Meech cheered and rushed off to go retrieve his girls. They were huddled backstage basking in the applause. "Y'all killed it! Come on! Dirt wants to meet you!"

The girls cheered, hugged and cheered some more before following Meech through the club. Heads turned when they got a glimpse of the girl group. Only, they turned away. Even the bouncer did a double take when they arrived at the rope. He had his instructions, so shrugged and let them in.

"And here they are! Dirt Jones meet T.K.K!" Meech happily introduced.

"Quit playing, cuz! Where the chicks at who was just singing?" Dirt asked as if this was some sort of joke. "Them girls sang too pretty to be this ugly!"

"Chill, Dirk!" Meech demanded and called him by his birth name. He knew the girls were ugly, but they were still people. Ugly people, but still people nonetheless, and you don't treat people like that.

"Dirt! He meant Dirt, Dirt Jones!" Dirt corrected but didn't correct his treatment of the girls. "Bruh, I can't do nothing with these mutts. I'ma give you one last shot to brang me an artist. You can tell grandma all you want!"

"Come on y'all," Meech said and led his girls away with long faces and lowered heads.

"Wow, he swaid we two wugly to swing," the bucktoothed girl moaned in her bucktooth language. Tears welled in the pot marks in Tosha's face while Kamala cried rivers in different directions from her cocked eyes. They all walked to the train together but Meech didn't

204

have money to board nor the courage to ask them to pay his fare.

"I'm sorry, guys, but it ain't over. I'ma get on sooner or later and I'ma put y'all on," he vowed.

"We know," Tosha sighed since she believed him. She couldn't do anything about their looks but knew they could sing. "Xscape made it and so can we!"

*****

Meech had to wait until the coast was clear and slid under the turnstile. He waited until he heard a train approaching and made a mad dash down the stairs. He had to turn sideways to beat the closing doors. He was almost ready to accept his fate of frying chicken on the night shift when he heard a wonderful noise. He turned his head and saw the source of the soulful singing.

Prince often sang for his dinner, the same way a fisherman puts a worm on a hook. He attracted both men and females with his crooning. This was Atlanta after all, so he wasn't surprised when saw saw Meech rushing towards him.

Prince loved chubby people like chubby people like deserts. That's probably why they had such a sweet taste to them. It was dinner and desert at the same time. They took a little longer in his crematorium but were reduced to ash, nonetheless.

"I'm finna make you a star!" Meech declared. He smiled and nodded along with himself to prove it.

"Original," Prince mused. He'd heard all kinds of pick up lines from males and females as he picked up both males and females. He preferred females so he could literally kill two birds with one stone. The girls he could fuck then suck. The guys just got drank.

"I'm serious! Look it!" he said and pulled up pictures of him and his cousin Dirt Jones. "See?"

"I see you on the train with me," Prince reminded. "Plus, some whack ass mumble rapper ain't exactly helping your cause. Check this..."

Meech felt a little light-headed when Prince began to rap. Especially when he realized it was a true freestyle based in real time about what was really around them. Even the stop on the train they arrived at. He was enjoying the show but still cut in and cut it off.

"Say no more! Mess with me and I'll make you rich and famous!" Meech swore. Dirt couldn't say anything about how it may look because chicks were sweating him from both ends of the car. A short, slim one batted her eyes, while a two hundred and fifty pounder giggled and waved.

Prince was amused and actually pretty curious. He seen the rap game evolved from the beginning in New York, then out to California. He'd always been on the sidelines so why not take center stage. Meech held his breath as Prince contemplated.

"I'on know," Prince said and stood as his stop approached. He nodded at big girl and she hopped to her feet instantly.

"Take my number. Call me. I'll make you famous," Meech pleaded. He knew Prince was the real deal. Plus, he really didn't want to have to go fry chicken all night.

"A'ight, I'll hit you up," he said and departed with his dinner and desert.

"Yes! Yes! Yes!" Meech cheered, jumped, and pumped his fist. Now he needed some minutes on his phone. He woke Angela up when he got home and gave her the business once more. He was on his way.

CHAPTER 22

"We finna kill this shit! You gonna be rich!" Meech cheered when Prince met him at the club.

"I am," Prince said confidently. "I perform better after I get my dick sucked."

"Um..." Meech paused. He wanted to be a full service manager but that was a bit much. "Man, I really don't, um...."

"Bruh," Prince laughed and shook his head at his dilemma but had other ideas.

A small flock of chickens in the line clucked for attention as they bypassed the line in favor of the VIP entrance. He inhaled the air and zoomed in on one of the girls. A heavily embellished, dark skinned girl who would have been prettier without the pounds of weave, makeup, and lashes. Her scent drove him wild and he had to have her.

"Bruh, we got a show to do," Meech whined when Prince waved the girls over.

"I know, and like I said, I perform better after I get my dick sucked," he repeated and selected a bird from the flock. "What's your name?"

"Shay," the girl giggled and blushed under her makeup and melanin. Meanwhile, Meech was worried since he knew he couldn't get all of these people in the VIP line. His, "they with me" had limits. Prince's didn't and he took the lead. The bouncer opened his mouth to dismiss the stranger and the ratchet girls but something else came out instead.

"They're with me," Prince said despite being unknown to him. To Meech's amazement, the man lifted the rope and let them all in. He did the same thing to another bouncer and took Shay into one of the dressing rooms like he was already a star.

Prince paused his hypnosis and tried to get into her mouth the old fashion way. They made out while his dick made its way into the picture and almost into her mouth.

"Say, Prince?" Meech called and knocked. "It's time to go!"

"Too, bad," Shay teased and twirled her tongue around his swollen dick head.

"I'll see you after the show," he said and led the way out of the room. He followed Meech backstage and got ready to turn the party out. That's exactly what he did when his turn came.

Prince came out and showed out. He sang and rapped to the stunned crowd. There was no surprise when Meech took him up to the VIP to meet his cousin Dirt Jones. They set an appointment for the following night and he took off in search of Shay.

"You were fiyah up there on stage!" Shay announced, setting off pre-fuck conversation. She wished she could have met him two days earlier before her cycle so she could get that hunk of meat inside of her. That was okay, though, because she planned to suck it so good, he would come back for more.

The conversation lasted until they pulled up to a rundown motel. He could afford more but it suited his needs. She had fucked here before and saw nothing wrong with it. A scruffy man saw the shiny car pull in and immediately moved on it.

Once inside, Prince sucked the flow like nectar of a ripe mango. Given the choice, he'd take blood over nectar any day. In fact, blood was the nectar he lived for. Shay began to moan and move as the sensation became sensational. An orgasm snuck up on her and shook her soul.

It was a going away present from the generous man. With a quick move, he turned and clamp onto her thigh. The super sharp fangs entered her flesh so smoothly, the pain took a few seconds to register.

"Motherfucker, is you biting me! Ow! stop!" she pleaded in futility. At that moment, he was a wild animal at feeding time. She tried to push his head away but couldn't. He brutally shoved her legs so wide her hips came out of their sockets with a sickening crunch. Panic set in and she began punching his head with both hands. "Get off me, nigga!"

The extra moving and thrashing played right into his plans. Her increased heartrate sped blood, coursing through her body that much quicker. Soon she felt light-headed from the loss of blood. He kept on sucking until she passed out. He kept right on going until she passed away.

"Delicious!" Prince told the corpse as a post mortem thanks. He stood and walked into the bathroom. After a quick shower, he dressed and stepped outside into the warm Atlanta night.

*****

"That nigga cuz brought through last night was the real deal!" Dirt announced.

"He was!" Matt agreed since that was his job. Every rapper has a hype man to cosign and hype whatever he says. A "yes man" to laugh at all the jokes and argue your point whether wrong or right. Matt was Dirt's.

"Shoot, I'm finna take that nigga from Meech. He 'ont know what to do with him," he said greedily. Every new artist and author gets jerked on their first deal and makes someone else rich. It's part of the game and a right of passage. As such, he wanted to pass it along and come up off the goldmine his cousin brought him. "I'll throw cuz like ten bands. He'll be a'ight."

"Word!" Matt concurred. He listened to his boss scheme on different ways to cheat Prince once he signed. Management fees, label imprint, hidden fees, parking, etc. He was going to TLC them like Pebbles did. Meanwhile, across town, Meech was worried.

*****

"Man, where he at? He ain't coming. That's fucked up!" Meech bitched and moaned, while watching the time on his phone. Prince had killed the showcase last night and they

211

were in. Now all they had to do was talk business and seal the deal. He had his whole spiel all mapped out from points, to tours, to merchandising. Little Dark Prince dolls for the kids, t-shirts, key chains, tennis shoes...

"Daydreaming at night?" Prince asked as he pulled up in his Lexus. Meech stood there blinking, trying to make sense of what he was seeing. Dude he met on the train had just pulled up in a Lambo, and that didn't make any damn sense.

"Um, I um. Can I even fit in that thing?" he asked when he got it together.

"Sure you can," Prince assured him and hit the door. It swung upwards, inviting him to a whole new life. Meech climbed in and took the offer.

Prince followed his directions until they pulled up to a midtown music studio. He parked next to Dirt's gaudy, tricked out SUV and they got out to go in.

"Hey, cuz! We was just talm'bout you. Want something to drank? Smoke?" Dirt offered eagerly.

"Hell yeah!" Meech accepted since his cousin never offered since he blew up. Prince partook, as well, even though neither had any affect. He couldn't quite read the man's thoughts but could still tell what was on his mind. He was going to cross his cousin first chance he got. Prince took a liking to Meech, and decided to ride with him. He had been around the business since the business began and easily spotted each lie Dirt told.

"How that sound?" Dirt asked after laying out his offer to manage, produce and sign to his imprint.

"Terrible!" Meech insisted. "I can do better selling out the trunk!"

"You need a car to sell out the trunk," Dirt reminded and turned to Prince.

"Now, you tryna hit the big leagues, so you need big league management!"

"I'm his manager!"Meech whined like he wanted to cry. He knew his cousin had the money and clout to steal his best prospect.

"You was. I'm finna give you ten grand to bow out," Dirt said and nodded at Matt.

"Bam!" Matt shouted theatrically and tossed the stack of money on the table in front of Meech.

"Take your money," Prince said. Meech didn't want to but couldn't stop himself. He turned to Dirt and informed him, "That's for his time. We can do everything you offered on our own and keep a lot more money. Holla back when you're serious."

"I, I, wait!" Dirt called after them as they left the room.

"Want me to bring him back?" Matt asked, as if he really could.

"Nah, he'll be back. I'll deal with cuz on it for a minute," Dirt relented. He would deal with Meech until he could get him out of his way. Even if he had to kill him.

Pretty much the same thing Prince was thinking. Except he would use Dirt to get established then make a sandwich out of him and his flunky. The rap world and beyond had no idea what was on the way. Get ready world, the Dark Prince has arrived.

*****

"Another one?" The mortician proclaimed when he processed Shay's shell. Prince got lazy and left the empty girl in the motel room. Plenty of bodies get discovered by the maids coming to swap out cum-crusted sheets and pillowcases.

This, however, was another one drained dry of blood. The two holes in the jugular veins got it added to a database of similar corpses across the country and around the world. A database monitored by vampire killers as well as something even more dangerous. Another vampire...

Stay tuned for part two but in the meantime, next up....

Dolla & Dyme: Jackin for Love

"Is that him?" Dolla asked, squinting through the dimly lit club. The ice on the target's neck illuminated him, putting him on his radar from all the way across the room. The dancer in front of him looked in the direction he was looking while still popping her caramel ass cheeks in his face.

"He shole look like the one," his equally ambitious partner Dyme said, licking her lips at the tasty lick in front of them. A good lick has a taste, and it's sweet. After wearing a three thousand dollar designer outfit and another ten around his neck, they were going to need a shot of insulin after this one. "It sure looks like him."

The mark must have wanted to get robbed when he pulled out a wad of cash and made it rain on the two dancers dancing in front of him. It was mainly ones and fives, but he still wouldn't have been doing it if he wasn't caked the fuck up. He could be charged as an accessory to his own robbery for flossing so hard. His Instagram post could be used against him in a court of law or holding court in the street.

"Yeah that's him, daddy," she purred like she does when her kitty is stroked. He wasn't supposed to be touching it since the club had a no touching policy but it was his pussy, so he would touch it when and where he wanted. "See, if I bust a nut on your hand, you gone swear I did you wrong."

"You do and I'm gonna bend you over this table and give you the business. All of it!" he warned and rolled his head back in laughter.

His bright smile contrasted brilliantly against his dark skin and turned heads. The same heads quickly turned back away since Dyme was quick to beat a bitch up over her man. He felt the same way and stopped fondling her when some locals watched him play in her pussy from a few tables over. He used the liquid she leaked to smooth the thick waves on his head since it worked better than Murrays.

"I'm down," she dared and would have done it if he wanted. Dolla was the first man to treat her right, so she was down for whatever he wanted. What he wanted now was to relieve all the cities clowns of their money. Dyme is what's known as a fine muthafucka. She stood five foot six inches and had an athletic body as in an ass as round as a basketball and firm breast the size regulation soft balls.

What set her apart from most of the highly made up strippers was she was naturally pretty. As pretty as she was, she was as rough as a dirt road. Her round face needed little embellishments to turn heads. A little lip-gloss on the thick lips beat all the beat faces in the club.

She further drove the value of her vagina up by not tricking with the ballers. Now they chunked bands at her to get her home and fuck. She accepted a few times, but they were the ones who got fucked. Fucked out of their money, drugs and jewels that is. Not one lived to tell about it.

"Nah, can't lose sight of buddy. Sic him," he laughed and sent her on her way with a slap on her ass.

The low budget ballers laughed at the display and earned and angry scowl from Dolla .He knew they were a problem when they kept staring at them in his native Brooklyn, New York eye contact that was considered a challenge. Staring could get you killed in the blink of an eye. An Atlanta, Georgia stare was slightly slower, so it took two blinks.

They proved his point when one of them reached for Dyme as she walked by. He could hear the music from The Omen when dude grabbed her wrist.

"Let us get a dance!" the spokesman insisted and tried to pull her close. She used a martial arts move and twisted herself out of his grip. Dolla knew his girl could handle it but stood just in case. He didn't bring a gun in but knew how to use a beer bottle as a club and knife if need be.

"Unhand me, nigga!" she fussed as she came free. She saw Dolla rise and knew she had seconds to defuse the situation before he lost his mind and blew the lick. "First of all, if all y'all malt liquor drinking niggas need one bitch for a table dance you can't afford me!"

"Ooohhh!" his partners jeered trying to get him to turn up. These were the type of broke goons who got into some shit everywhere they went. They got into more fights than into a woman, so the strip club was as close as they came to some pussy.

Dyme beat her feet and put some distance between them before security or Dolla intervened. Security would have evicted their asses from the club. Dolla would have evicted their souls from their bodies.

"Fuck you looking at?" the spokesman dared when he saw Dolla looking their way.

"My bad, shawty," he said like a local and raised his hand in surrender. This wasn't the time nor place for confrontation, so he put it in reverse. He summoned a waitress with his hand that sent them a round of drinks on him. It was the least he could for the condemned men. They didn't know it yet, but their last meal was their last meal.

"Damn! Who the fuck is that bitch?" Po-boy asked the stripper working in front of him when Dyme sashayed through the VIP section.

Her round ass did its little dance as she walked without even trying. She had a naturally nasty walk that she couldn't turn off if she wanted to. It could turn up, down a little, but never off. Po-boy got his name as a skinny child but never changed it even he got his weight.

His financial weight that is because the six-footer was still rail thin with large eyes that made him look like a cartoon character. He really was poor coming up and couldn't afford to keep a chick. He made up for it now by tricking almost every night.

"Her name is Dyme, but she ain't gone fuck," Diamond replied and shook her ass a little harder. She couldn't stand Dyme's pretty ass since should had to fuck and suck these salty dicks to compete with what the pretty girl could make just from dancing. She had to wear so much makeup and wigs to fake being pretty that she resembled a transvestite.

A few guys actually thought she was a dude when they took her home only to be disappointed she was really a girl in boy shorts and not a boy. This was Atlanta after all.

"All bitches fuck if the price right! Call her over here," he said and shoved some cash at her to send her on her way.

"Bitch ass nigga," she fussed as she went to carry out her mission. She stepped back into her boy shorts and rushed to catch up. "Yo, Dyme . That nigga with the ice want you. We can take this nigga to the motel and work a band out his ass!"

"We?" Dyme laughed at the attempt to be down. The veteran stripper made it known she wanted a taste when Dyme first started working here. Either her or the owner Ant got to sample all the products. All except Dyme that is.

"I'm saying tho. You know these trick niggas be wantin' to see some freaky shit!

219

They spend more money to see two gals," she explained. She and Ant had a standing bet to see who fucked her first, so she wouldn't take no for answer.

"Hell naw," she said since the regular "no" didn't get it. She looked over at Po-boy and scrunched her face up like he was ugly then turned away. The snub drove her stock even higher.

"Told you she be on that bullshit. Shit, I'll grab any other one of these hoes to come with us. We'll freak yo' skinny ass out!" Diamond dared and lolled out her tongue to show off her well-used tongue ring.

It touched as much pussy as dicks since she went both ways and sideways. She was a true tri-sexual who would try almost anything sexual.

"Her!" Po-boy cheered, pointing at Desire. She was his first choice until Dyme sauntered by. He may not have gotten her tonight, but vowed he had to have her.

Dyme threw up one finger towards her man as she entered the dressing room. He understood it um mean "one minute" as she dressed in her street clothes. He hoped it didn't take much longer since the club was closing and he had one last thing to do before they retired for the night.

"You ready?" Dyme asked as if it were she who had been waiting on him. She looked just as sexy in the short skirt as she did in stripper clothes.

"Yeah, come on!" he urged and rushed her towards the exit. He spotted who he was looking for just as they pulled from the parking lot. Dyme saw them too and smiled. People always talk about the murder but not the fuck shit that prompted it. These dudes were disrespectful and were about to get disrespected in the worse way.

"You drive!" Dolla said and went to retrieve the long bag from the trunk. He came around to the passenger seat but Dyme had beat him to it. He could only shake his head and handed her the bag.

"Here."

Dolla came back around and jumped behind the wheel. She pointed left in the direction of their prey and he pulled out after them. Meanwhile, she got the grill ready for the cookout. He smiled at the sexy sound of her racking a round into the AR 15 submachine gun. It had a modified stock that let it rip almost fully automatic. It could empty the 100 round clip in seconds. She removed the safety and waited on her shot to take shots.

"We'll catch 'em on Griffin Street," he said as they bent a corner. She rolled down her window as he closed the distance between them. They made it easy when the driver pulled to sudden stop when he saw Rabbit waving at cars. Her head game was the stuff of legend. She could make quick work of the four dicks in four minutes and get another blast.

"Suck a nigga dick or something," the driver proposed. It was his car, which meant he had first on her tongue. Rabbit opened her mouth to name her price until she saw Dyme rolled out the passenger window and up the rifle. The men all turned to see whatever made her eyes go wide as a hit of the cities finest dope. None of them liked what they saw.

"Oh..." would be the last words the driver got to utter in this life before she blasted him into the next.

The "shit" that was to follow would have to wait until he got to hell. The gun looked more like a flamethrower as it threw round after round into the car. The men in back tried um duck behind the door but the heavy 5.56 rounds didn't give a fuck about a car door. They ripped through it them and out the other side.

The front passenger made a break for it but didn't get far. He only made it a few feet before a shot to his back knocked a lung out his chest. She gunned Rabbit down as an afterthought so she could never testify.

"Yo, that shit was dope!" Dolla said as he pulled from the curb. He mashed the gas and put some distance between them and the murder scene. That shit made my dick hard!

"Nuh uh!" Dyme dared and reached for his crotch. Sure enough, it was as hard as a scorned woman's heart. She knew just what to do with a hard dick and leaned in to do it.

"Shit," Dolla said as her hot mouth welcomed him inside.

Her slow stroke, kiss, lick, suck, had him fucked up and he knew they wouldn't make it good. He reached under her skirt and played and played in her puddle and they both knew they wouldn't make it to their suburban hideaway.

Dyme giggled when he snatched the car to a dark on a dark street. He pulled her on top of him and slid her thong aside. She shoved her whole tongue his mouth as he wriggled himself inside of her.

"Shit!" she cussed from the pain his pleasure always brought. She decided to make him feel it took and bit his bottom lip.

"Grrr," he growled from the taste of blood in his mouth. He palmed the basketball-sized cheeks and bounced them up and down on his dick. The smell of fresh gunpowder mixed with the sounds of her splashing juice box and drove the both wild.

"Mmm, that's it. Get it," she urged even though he was hurting her. His guttural grunts signaled the end was near. She gripped the headrest and threw her hips into overdrive.

Dolla 's whole body seized and shivered when he began sending a torrent of semen into her. He leaned up and matched her kisses until the spasms of orgasms subsided.

"Whew!" he exclaimed when his breathing returned to normal. He patted her ass signaling her to get up. She did and fell over into the passenger seat. His dick was still too hard to put up so he drove off with it still out.

"You know I ain't done, right?" she said wickedly.

"I'll pull over again if you want," he dared. Would have too, but she declined.

"Nah, I need some space," she said and leaned back for the ride. She rode him backwards once they got back to the room. They made love until the crack of dawn and finally got some rest. They were going to need for their next lick.